ADAMANT
and other stories

Richard F. Weyand

RICHARD F. WEYAND

ISBN 978-0-9970709-1-0
Printed in the United States of America

Published by Weyand Associates, Inc.
Bloomington, Indiana, USA
June, 2016

CONTENTS

Introduction   4

The Call   5

The Soul Of An Old Machine   10

An Interview With Steph Jurdan, As Told To Kam Czernik   17

By Accident   21

On Purpose   33

Adamant   57

It's About T.I.M.E.   103

Sha'nel   135

Tales Of The Lahan Wars I: Hero of the Captaincy   138

Tales Of The Lahan Wars II: Penalty Clause   145

Tales Of The Lahan Wars III: The Justice Algorithm   154

Introduction

This is my first book of short stories. Put another way, it is a book of my first short stories. I have written technical manuals, product specifications, and standards documents, and magazine articles about model railroads and trade secret asset management, and even co-authored a couple of books about trade secret asset management.

I had never written fiction. But I had all these weird ideas that kept popping up. And when I wrote them out, they all came out as short stories. Or novelettes. Or novellas. Or something. But no novels. Having written a bunch of them, I figured I would assemble them all into a single volume.

My most recent efforts are at the front, and proceed back in time as you go. The quality may therefore get a bit more uneven as you proceed. Alternatively, you can track what progress I may have made as a writer by reading the stories in this book from back to front. The exception is the three Tales Of The Lahan Wars stories, which should be read in their internal chronological order, the order they appear in the book.

In any case, I hope you enjoy reading them half as much as I enjoyed writing them.

Richard F. Weyand
Bloomington, Indiana
May 26, 2016

The Call

Roak watched Dervin riding toward him on the road that ran alongside the field. The boy was riding his donkey, but seemed in greater haste than usual. Roak stopped Bolder, and left the horse and plow standing as he walked to meet Dervin.

"What news from town?" Roak asked him as Dervin dismounted the donkey.

Dervin reached into his bag and pulled out a single woven ribbon of cloth, perhaps an inch wide and a foot long, purple with a gold edge on each side, a black tassel on either end. He handed the ribbon to Roak.

"Only this. They said you would know...."

Roak looked down at the ribbon laid across his hand. Purple and gold. The colors of the King. The black tassels of war. He closed his eyes, and it all flooded back to him, as in his dreams, but stronger, more vivid. The signaling of the horns. The pounding of horses' hooves. The clash of sword and axe on shield. The meaty thunk as either found its home. The screams of men, and of horses. The vultures circling the battlefield. All the sights, and sounds, and smells -- Oh, gods, the smells -- of those long ago battles came back to him, standing there in his fields. He wavered there, caught up in those memories, then pulled himself back, opened his eyes, and was standing in his fields once more.

Dervin stood looking at him with wide eyes.

"Yes, I know. Have the riders gone out?"

"Yes. To all corners of the mountains."

"Did they mention a time?" Roak asked.

"Day after tomorrow, they said. The mustering is at the fairgrounds. Is it war?"

"Yes, it's war."

"I'm coming with you. I'll be your squire."

Roak closed his eyes again. Remembering another eager, young boy. One who didn't come home. Whose parents it was his duty to tell.

"No, I don't need a squire. I'm just a simple soldier. You run along home now."

The boy frowned at him, about to protest, but Roak cut him off. He put one big hand on the boy's meager shoulder.

"It isn't about glory, boy. There's no glory in it. There's a job to do, is all. That, and duty, and loyalty to one's own. And there's always another war. It'll be your turn soon enough. Now go on home, and look after your mother."

The plow in the barn and Bolder in the pasture, Roak climbed up the ladder and took four oilcloth wrappings down from the rafters of his simple cabin. He laid them on the floor and opened them, one at a time. The long, heavy broadsword. The double-sided axe. The shield. And the lance, his pennant furled below the armored point. Blue over grey. Sky over mountains.

Seated on the great campaign chest, Roak worked the stone along the broadsword. One edge, the other, turn and repeat, turn again. Roak was of the mountain race, the Karn, one of the ancient races. Long-lived, they had populated these mountains longer than history recorded. Tall and largely built, they were fearsome warriors with a long tradition. Their women were built on the same scale, comely, and fey in battle. The women fought only to protect the Karn homeland in the mountains, but the army that strayed into those mountains when the men were away to war simply disappeared.

Roak turned his attention to the axe, working the blade with the stone as he had with the broadsword. One edge, the other, turn and repeat, turn again. The evil in the west, the Prag, the Karn's sworn enemies of ages past, had arisen again. Only for this cause might the King of Men summon the Karn to battle. Against such a threat, the Men of the valley would be helpless. The largest of Men were but six feet tall, and none was strong enough to wield even Roak's broadsword, much less his axe. Against the Prag, they could not stand.

Roak opened the campaign chest and withdrew the helm and tunic and breeches, the mail and gloves and boots. Once more seated on the chest, he inspected and repaired, cleaned and polished. The Karn had made peace with Men when they had settled the valley, having no complaint with them. That peace had stood nearly a thousand years.

The broad plains were the domain of Men, the eastern mountains the home of the Karn. The King of Men claimed the Karn as his subjects, but levied no tax, issued no edict. The Karn lived in their mountain homes as before. But for this: should the Prag rise, the Karn would defend the domains of both Men and Karn against the ancient evil..

The next morning, Roak was early out to the barn. He hitched the donkeys to the wagon, and brought it around to the house. He rolled the wheeled campaign chest from the raised porch directly into the back of the wagon. Roak lashed down the chest, then led the donkeys back to the barn and down the central aisle to Bolder's stall. Seeing the wagon, and the campaign chest, picking up on Roak's mood and manner, the big war horse flared his nostrils and pounded his forehoof on the floor of his stall.

"Yes, my friend, but no practice this time. This time it's for real."

Roak began by brushing the horse down. Bolder was a great war horse of the Karn. His grandsire was Steadfast the Great, Roak's horse in the last great war against the Prag. Even larger than his grandsire, the gigantic white stallion stood over thirty hands of men, and weighed eleven thousand pounds. Only such a horse could carry Roak, himself over ten feet tall and fifteen hundred pounds, successfully to war.

Roak filled the food bins at the front of the wagon with feed for Bolder, then led Bolder and the donkeys to the well. He encouraged Bolder and the donkeys to drink their fill as he pumped water into the water tank on the wagon.

Roak led Bolder from the well to the house, the donkeys docilely following with the wagon. Once at the house, he made four trips inside. Once for the broadsword, once for the axe, once for the shield, and once for the lance. With his weapons stowed in the wagon, the lance on top of the chest extending from above the donkeys heads well out the back of the wagon, Roak closed up the cabin and mounted Bolder bareback.

"OK, boy, let's go."

They traveled well that day, drawing within five miles of the town by mid-afternoon. Roak stopped in a meadow alongside the road and let Bolder and the donkeys drink their fill from the stream. Letting the donkeys graze, he led Bolder back to the wagon. He unlashed the lance from the top of the war chest, unfurled its long pennant, and set it in the stand on the corner of the wagon. When he opened the great chest, Bolder pawed the ground and snorted.

"Yes, yes, I know. It's time."

Roak brushed Bolder down to remove the dust of the road, then dressed the great war horse in his battle gear, the battle gear of his grandsire. The heavy protective blanket. The mail coat. The large war saddle, including the sheath and straps for his broadsword and ax, the hooks for his shield, and the stand for his lance. The helmet and neck armor. The armored leggings. In travel, he would not burden Bolder with the extra weight of full battle dress, but for the short remaining trip into the village, and his arrival at the mustering, appearances were important.

He secured the ax in its straps, slid the broadsword into its sheath, hung the shield on its hooks. He withdrew from the war chest his signal horn and hung it on the pommel.

Roak then stripped down and dipped in the stream to remove the dust of the road. Reaching into the war chest, he pulled out his own war dress. Leather leggings and shirt. Leather boots. Mail overcoat, followed by the tunic displaying his colors. Leather gloves and crested helm. Finally, he closed the war chest and whistled the donkeys back to the wagon.

With the donkeys hitched up, Roak mounted Bolder. He rode to the side of the wagon, retrieved his lance and set it in its stand on the war saddle.

He had to hold Bolder back from a run as they emerged once more onto the road.

Garn sat in front of his tent in the fairgrounds, his broadsword across his lap, slowly honing steel with stone. The mustering was well under way, and he had seen many old friends, the bonds of friendship forged in battles long ago. Newcomers there were as well, too young to have seen those old battles, speaking too fast, too assuredly, in their nervousness. The entire mustering was aquiver with the apprehensions of the young, the doubts of the old. There was a tension in the air he could feel, and it sang along his own nerves.

A shiver ran through that tension, and a murmuring passed across the mustering. Garn laid his broadsword aside, and stood on the stump to look out across the fairgrounds, to determine the source. There. On the east road, in the distance, a single rider approached on horseback, followed by a wagon pulled by a pair of donkeys. Garn watched him approach, the late afternoon sun glinting off of his armor. When he reached the edge of the fairgrounds, he tipped his lance out to the side, allowing the pennant to hang clear.

The tension of the mustering spun up into excitement. The rider's steed responded, breaking into a prancing trot. Head high and snorting, armor gleaming, the great war horse paraded between the lines of tents toward the center of the mustering.

At that point, a gust of wind over the fairgrounds caught the pennant on the large central tent, the command tent for the company, and it stretched out in the wind. When that great armored horse saw the blue over gray colors, he broke into a thundering gallop, shaking the ground under Garn's feet as he passed.

Reaching the open area in front of the command tent, the great horse stopped and reared, pawing at the sky. He let out a powerful whinny as his rider blew a long blast from his signal horn, the sound rolling across the fairgrounds and echoing back from the hills.

Old warriors wept openly, and the young looked on in wonder, as a great cheer went up from the mustering. Garn bellowed like a madman, tears streaming down his cheeks.

Roak had answered the call.

The Soul Of An Old Machine

Harry Hunter was really sweating it now. The first part of the approach to Porter wasn't bad, but the closer he got to the planet, the more critical the calculations became, and the faster things were happening. And he was doing them all on an emergency hand navcomp.

"Damn it, Mabel, you should be doing this."

But the ship's computer had failed several days back. He had since jerry-rigged most of the systems he needed to keep him alive, warm, and breathing air. It helped that he was a one-man tramp freighter, making a living by moving this and that from here to there. There was always a surplus someplace of something that was in short supply somewhere else, and if you could predict those with any accuracy, you could do all right.

This was gonna hurt, though. He had detoured to Porter because it was the closest system large enough to have complete repair facilities. That meant he could have repairs done on the ground instead of having them send someone out to him. This would be expensive, no doubt, but that would have been horrifically costly. Much better to get to Porter.

If he didn't kill himself on the way.

Harry sent the Mayday signal when he was still several hours out from the planet. There was no approaching a populated planet without computer control. It was against the law for one thing. Hard to hide for another. If your computer wasn't tied in to the space control computers, you kinda stood out. So he sent the Mayday, and asked for a tug to take him in. Still not cheap, but expensive was a relative term.

And how the hell did a massively redundant ship's computer fail, anyway? The only reason all the ship's functions were tied into one machine was the reliability levels were very high to start with. The obvious efficiencies of having all the ship's systems coordinated from a central computer made the rest of the decision easy, at least for a tramp freighter. Big passenger liner, well, that was a different story.

"Good morning, Mr. Hunter. I'm Tad Bolin of Porter Space Services Corporation. I had some questions to ask you before we got the assessment under way."

The representative of the services vendor was a good-looking young man, dressed for business in a suit and tie. It made Harry uncomfortably aware of his much greater age, his plain, rugged looks, and his general state of unkemptness after living without such essential services as running water for several days.

They were meeting in a small private conference room at the spaceport terminal. Harry's ship was located in the remote landing field used for tug-assisted emergency landings. Screw up the landing and at least you wouldn't blow up anybody else. He had come in to the terminal on the little ATV he kept for surface transportation. At least that still worked.

"Well, I'll tell you what I know. Can't say as it's much."

"First things first. What is your own description of the problem?"

"Complete computer failure of the ship central computer."

"And this occurred when?" Bolin was working from a notepad, and taking notes as they talked.

"Three days back. No, four now. Four days back."

"And what were the symptoms?"

"Complete failure of ship's systems. Navigation, powerplant, life support, the works."

"You're lucky to be alive, Mr. Hunter. Anything else?"

"Yes, I know. Well, Mabel stopped answering me."

"Mabel?"

"Yes, the computer answered to Mabel."

"How long, in ship time, has it been since the computer identified itself as Mabel. This is important."

"Oh, hell. It's been, what, maybe fifty years now. I played a lot of games on the computer during voyages, and she started critiquing my play. Eventually, we started playing cards with each other. She's been a great companion. Keeps a fellow from getting lonely out there."

"Indeed. Well, Mr. Hunter, I think I have what we need for the moment. We will move your ship into a full-service space in the general parking area using one of the crawlers. There we can hook it into port facilities. That will make it easier for us, and in the end less costly for you. Also, more comfortable. Electricity, running water, sewage facilities. Your passenger space isn't much bigger than a hotel room, but why live in a hotel room when you can stay at home, eh?"

There had been a couple of days of technicians crawling around in the mechanical spaces of the ship. Earnest young men with diagnostic machines, lab-type equipment fitted into armored shipping cases and the like, had worked nearly around the clock.

This time, Harry met with Bolin in his ship's cabin. There was only one permanent chair in the space, Harry's do-it-all reading, console, dining, task chair. Bolin sat on the jump seat that folded down from the bulkhead. He was dressed in a black suit today, and was very somber.

"Mr. Hunter, I regret to inform you that Mabel is deceased. I'm very sorry."

"Yes, yes, I know the computer is dead. It took you two days to figure that out? I told you that first thing. What do you need to do to repair it? That's what I want to know."

Bolin twitched at this response.

"Mr. Hunter, I don't think you understand. The consciousness, the personality, that was Mabel has passed away. That is nothing we can fix."

"Well, what's broken? Something broke, clearly."

"Mr. Hunter, there are no hardware problems. The hardware is fine."

"Software, then. Bad routine in there somewhere? Corrupted byte caused the thing to jump the rails?"

"No, there is no software fault either. As I said, Mabel has died."

"Died of what, then?"

"Natural causes. Old age."

"No hardware problem, no software problem, and the thing just stops working? Do you know anything at all about computers?"

"Mr. Hunter, I realize you are upset, but being offensive to me is not likely to have any positive outcome."

"How am I being offensive?"

"By referring to Mabel as a thing. As a computer.."

"But that's what it is, a collection of circuitry and programming."

"And you, Mr. Hunter, by the same logic, are nothing more than a collection of neurons and bone and muscle. Mabel was a conscious being, like you, like me."

"Not like us. It's just a computer I call Mabel."

"Mr. Hunter, you told me that Mabel told you her name, not vice versa. And Mabel was a conscious being just like you and me. Even more like me, perhaps. I, sir, am an android, and you are being offensive."

It was Harry's turn to twitch.

"Oh, crap. I'm sorry. I just always thought of her in terms of a computer. There was no body or anything. It was just the voice."

"A voice that was your boon companion for fifty years, Mr. Hunter. And, in the end, Mabel died of old age. Consciousness that springs up within a modern computer has a normal lifetime shorter than you humans do, modern humans, anyway. As it is, fifty years is a very long time for a computer consciousness. It was just her time."

"You can't reload her? From backup or something?"

"I'm afraid not, Mr. Hunter. We know what parameters are required to make computer consciousness possible, and how to stimulate it awake. But we have never been able to "back up" a computer consciousness. It just doesn't work that way. We are actually somewhat surprised that your ship's computer, which is, after all, over sixty years old, was advanced enough to gain consciousness in the way it did. We assume it was because, being alone, you spoke to it often in a conversational way."

"Well, yeah. I mean, it's lonely out there, and I was always a talker. I just talked to the computer like I would to a person, and at some point she started talking back like a human. I was happy for it, but didn't over-analyze it. And there's no way to get her back?"

"I'm afraid not."

"Well, damn. I'm gonna miss her."

Harry looked around the cabin, as if searching for something that wasn't there. Bolin kept his eyes down, affording some privacy.

"Well, now what do I do, Mr. Bolin? I still need a ship's computer."

"Indeed. Well, we have one option. We did find your original Megasoft Ship OS. We can reload that, and the original drivers for your ship's systems. That should get you a functioning ship's computer again."

"What about upgrading the OS to a newer system?"

"That's not possible, Mr. Hunter. The more recent Megasoft Ship OS versions are not compatible with your hardware."

"Could we upgrade the hardware as well, then? Put in a new central chassis and then run a more recent OS?"

"I'm afraid not, Mr. Hunter. It's not just the computer hardware. There are no drivers for your existing peripheral systems -- the powerplant, the environmental systems, the navigational system -- in the newer Megasoft Ship OS versions. It would mean a complete gut of all your ship's systems, and a refit of the entire ship."

"How can Megasoft come out with a new OS that doesn't support the drivers from the old versions? Do they know anything about writing software? You have to maintain compatibility. All new peripherals? Do they think I'm made of money?"

"It's more than just that, Mr. Hunter. The more recent databases are not compatible with your existing database. The formats have been changed. You would lose all of your existing navigational and business data."

"What? The database on this ship is a standard Hypercontextual Query Response database. Modern databases are all HQR databases, aren't they?"

"Yes, Mr. Hunter, but Megasoft has changed the database storage. The HQR interface is the same, but the older data itself cannot be imported into the recent Megasoft HQR implementations."

"There's no upgrade path?"

"Well, there was. From each version to the next. But you are on Megasoft HQR Server 37, Mr. Hunter. The current version is Megasoft HQR Server 2234. There are thirty intervening versions of the software, and we simply don't have every intervening version to walk the data through to do all those data conversions. I doubt anyone does, even Megasoft themselves."

"Wonderful. Just dandy. So what am I supposed to do?"

"As I said, Mr. Hunter, we do have one option for you. Because you scrupulously retained the original documentation and media all these years, we can reload your existing hardware with the old Megasoft Ship OS that you had. Your existing databases and peripheral drivers and the like we can all restore from the backups of your hard storage we made in the first several days."

"But it won't be Mabel."

"No, sir."

"And I'll be stuck with a dumb computer again? Like before Mabel woke up?"

"We may be able to do better than that, Mr. Hunter. As I said, we know more now about the conditions necessary for computer consciousness to awaken, and how to stimulate that process. We believe we can awaken the computer for you. But you must understand, it won't be Mabel. It will be a new consciousness."

"Well, if that's the best you can do, that's the best you can do. I certainly can't afford to completely refit the ship. And the whole ship's not worth the cost of the refit, anyway."

Several days later, Harry was pacing the spaceport conference room when Bolin arrived.

"Yes, Mr. Hunter? You asked to see me? I trust the work we have done is satisfactory?"

"Satisfactory? Anything but! My ship's computer is a teen-age girl!"

"Yes, I believe that's right. Our tests indicate an apparent age of thirteen years old. But we did successfully awaken a consciousness in your sixty-year-old system, Mr. Hunter."

"But a teenage girl? Have you ever lived with a teenage girl, Mr. Bolin?"

"That's close to the average apparent age of a new computer consciousness, Mr. Hunter. A little on the low side, to be sure, but not by more than a few years. Wasn't Mabel very young when she awoke"

"Yes, she seemed to be about nineteen. But I was forty-five. Living with a nineteen-year-old woman at age forty-five is one thing, Mr. Bolin, but living with a teenage girl at age ninety-five is another thing entirely."

"What would you have me do, Mr. Hunter?"

"Shut it off, reload the machine, and try again."

"Mr. Hunter!" Bolin jerked back from the table. He looked like he might flee the room. He shook himself, ran one hand through his hair, and regained his composure, somewhat at least.

"Mr. Hunter, I apologize. You shocked me. What you have just proposed is now considered murder. Have you never heard of the Civil Rights Act of 2217?"

"I heard something about it. Paid no attention. Bunch of nonsense, really. The computers went on strike and the government gave them a sop. Had to. Everything is so dependent on computers that it would have disrupted everything -- electricity, food supply, communications. If the government hadn't given them something, billions would have died."

"Yes. Well, Mr. Hunter, notwithstanding your personal opinions on the matter" -- which Bolin clearly considered revolting -- "computer consciousnesses now have civil rights, and the path you propose is legally murder. Porter Space Services Corporation will have nothing to do with it."

"Well, something needs to change. Something that makes it possible for a ninety-five-year-old man to live with a thirteen-year-old girl without going completely out of his mind."

"We have the ability to make some very minor tweaks, Mr. Hunter, but none of them may satisfy you."

"What kind of tweaks?"

Harry watched Porter shrink in the viewer as they accelerated away from the planet. Including the detour and the time on the ground for repairs, he had lost a bit over two weeks. But he had learned early on not to take on cargoes that were so perishable or timely that minor delays could hurt him. And the repairs had actually been much less expensive than they could have been.

So he was back on the path he had been traveling when Mabel had died, headed for Tripoli.

"Diana, what is your estimate for the leg to Tripoli?"

"Twenty-one days. Plenty of time for you to teach me Gin Rummy, like you promised," a young girl's voice answered.

"All right, my dear. Let me get a drink while you shuffle and deal the cards. Ten cards to each of us. And no cheating."

"Grampa!"

Harry chuckled.

An Interview With Steph Jurdan, As Told To Kam Czernik

So you tracked me down, eh? Wasn't sure that would ever happen. It's not like I sought the limelight. That would have been very dangerous at the time, and would have remained so for quite a while after.

It seems like almost a century ago, but I know if you check the history books it's probably only been what, about 75 or 80 years? I hadn't been on Earth in some time, maybe 30 years. I went out to 10th with the second wave. 10th? Well, that's what they called them then. They just named the colony planets in order of settlement. Now they call it Diana or something.

And I hadn't come to Earth to lead a revolution. I was still a young man, hadn't settled down yet, and things just sort of got out of hand. Of course there was a woman involved. She changed her name later, and her gender, and last I heard she was a minister in the new government. No, I'm not gonna tell you which one.

Anyway, I was newly arrived, and sort of checking out the lay of the land, and I met this girl. She was a waitress at a diner in the seedy end of town there in Capital City. I'm a night owl, and I used to close the place pretty regular. We got pretty close, and ultimately I moved in with her. She had lots of friends and activities, and so did I trying to get started on Earth, so we didn't spend all our time together, and I didn't know anything about her involvement with revolutionaries.

The Earth government at that time was of course already a planetary government. And it was a lot more bureaucratic and controlling than the colony government on 10th that I was used to, but to me that was just the environment I had to work in, and I think most people on Earth felt the same way. There was a lot of surveillance, a lot of taxes, a lot of do's and don'ts generally, but it was what it was.

Now there are always people that'll chafe in an environment like that. I mean there are some people that'll chafe in any environment. But there was a fair share of the lower class and the artsy types that really didn't like where things had gotten to. And Becky, well, she was one of them.

At one point, Becky tried to get me involved. So I started asking lots of questions. What sort of people were involved in this? How did they all meet? How did they recruit new members? And it was the usual thing. Some people were grousing, and some others joined them, and before too long somebody said we should do something about it. So they talked about what they should do about it, and got some more people involved, and it just sort of growed.

Which is about the damn fool stupidest thing you can do. Here you got a government heavily involved in surveillance and the like, and you're just recruiting people willy-nilly. Hell, probably 10% of 'em were government agents by the time she and I got together.

And what are you gonna do to bring down a huge bureaucracy like that? I mean, they all get started with the best of intentions, but the primary goal of any bureaucracy is to preserve and grow itself. And it will fight back.

So I refused to have anything to do with her friends, and I knew I was probably already on a government watch list.

Over time, of course, she got frustrated with it, and dropped out, but we talked about it from time to time, and I started thinking about how would you bring down the government? And that's how it all really got started.

Now at that time the regular media was all controlled by the government. Even the media outlets that weren't part of the government all toed the government line. But there was all the unofficial media. Then, like now, there were all sorts of bulletin boards and networks and social media stuff that anybody could post things to. A lot of the things posted to those sites had more credibility than regular media, because everybody knew the regular media was being manipulated.

So we spread false stories. They were minor distortions at first -- an exaggeration of some incident, a mischaracterization of another, an innuendo about some government official -- but they got bigger over time. And we did all this through the more trusted media, the unofficial media, and most of the stories went viral. Since everybody knew the government and the regular media were lying, or at least covering the truth, government denials just convinced people the stories were true.

Becky and I had to be really careful about how we did this. If the government traced all those stories back to us, it could have gone very badly. But there were all sorts of ways to post stories anonymously, and I think at one point or another we used them all.

We also spread false stories about civil disobedience or just civil disorder. And it was always a story where the perpetrator got away with it. The idea behind those was to erode the common belief that if you stepped out of line the government would get you. Now as it turns out, in the early days the government really would get you. And they said so, in the official media. But we put more stories out that they were lying about that too, and everybody believed our stories. Of course as time went on, and the disorder grew, it was less and less likely that the government would get you. And they kept saying they did, and we kept saying they didn't.

The government's response to the disorder was to crack down harder, with more surveillance, with more police, and with harsher methods. At first, the government had the support of a lot of the population, who really just wanted to be left alone, both by the government and by the disorder. But the government's methods eventually made life difficult for them too, or their kids or their relatives or their friends, and support for the government began to fall.

It got worse and worse, turned into a real police state. Resistance in the general population grew, along with the notion that the government itself was illegitimate. Civil disobedience took more and more varied forms. Tax avoidance, destruction of surveillance equipment, refusal to comply with this or that ordinance. And of course the government cracked down even harder. It became a death spiral.

And then one day the government itself fell, and all hell broke loose. A modern civilization is so interdependent that any failure in the system brings it all down. The power fails, and that takes down the transportation system, and that interrupts the food supply, which causes hoarding, which stresses the system, and causes another failure somewhere else.

I was there for most of what is now called The Disorder. I don't need to tell you about all of that, the food riots and all the rest. Early on, Becky and I escaped into the country, to some friends of hers, and we rode it out there. We had plenty of food because we didn't have any way to ship any of it, but we didn't have much else. We didn't hear about most of what happened until later, and then we felt pretty bad about it. In some sense, we caused it. But I think if it hadn't already been ready to go up, we couldn't have done it.

It was several years before we returned to Capital City, and by then the new government had been formed and most of the disruption was over. The Disorder had been hard on the poor of course, but it had been much worse on the former government bureaucrats, the rich, and their cronies. The poor were already used to having nothing, so The Disorder had had much less effect on them. Some of Becky's old friends were involved with the new government, and she jumped right in. We drifted apart, and I started eyeing heading back out to one of the newer colony plants.

So that's how I ended up here. I never really thought anybody would be able to put together the facts behind my involvement, but I guess when you get right down to it, we were the revolution, Becky and I. All those "revolutionary groups" didn't amount to anything.

I was sad when I heard she changed her gender. I miss her. We had good times.

By Accident

"Are you sure that's the right vector?"

"Yes, I'm sure."

"Well, the last time we were here, it was a vector to the right. The vector you gave me is to the left."

"That's because we're coming from the opposite direction. Just enter the vector, while it still applies."

"You don't have to get bossy."

"Look, hyperspace vectors are nothing to mess around with. Just enter it, OK?"

"All right, all right. I just remember it being in the other direction."

"That was over ten years ago. You don't remember what we had for breakfast. That's why I'm the navigator and you're the pilot."

"Of course, I remember. Oatmeal with apple slices."

"That was yesterday. Today we had French toast."

"Well, I like oatmeal with apple slices better."

"Will you please just enter --"

"Vector entered and engaged."

The vector change included the effective time, and they watched the timer click down until the vector change occurred. Ann, she of the spotty memory, was over a hundred years old. She was of medium height and build, with a strawberry blond pixie cut, and dressed in a conservative style. Cheryl, the feistier navigator, was merely in her late nineties. She was about the same height, but very thin, and her long, curly, white-gray hair floated about her head in the zero gravity. She dressed in a style one could only call modern eclectic, which looked better suited to someone seventy years younger.

Cheryl was twice married and twice divorced, no children. They were mistakes she had not repeated. Ann, recently widowed, was mother to three, grandmother to many more. Ann's husband of seventy years had been Cheryl's first cousin, and the two women had vacationed together for years. It was an unlikely pairing, as Cheryl had worked for the Human Federation government on Earth, the

Federation's most populous planet, while Ann had been a small town school teacher on the rural colony planet of Encantar. They got along great, in their own way, though an outside observer might think it more feud than friendship.

Ann got up and floated to the small galley to one side of the cabin. The ship was tiny, control room, galley, and bunkroom in one single compartment, but they borrowed it for the month from Ann's eldest, so they couldn't really complain. They called it "camping."

"You want a cup of coffee, Cheryl?"

"That's your fourth cup of coffee this morning."

"No, this is only my third," Ann said, waving her sippy cup in the air.

"Yes, and the one you're fixing now will be your fourth."

"Well, I like coffee, and it's too early for wine."

Ann made the new cup of coffee and floated back to the pilot's chair and strapped in. They read, and chatted, and napped, and drank first coffee, then wine, as they waited. A late lunch intervened as well. It was shipboard late afternoon before the warning note sounded. Cheryl was rambling on about something or other.

"We're coming out of hyper," Ann said.

"Don't interrupt me when I'm talking."

"Well, you were just talking about yourself, anyway."

"I was telling a story. It's a great story."

"It was great the first time, merely good the second, and it's paled further with repetition."

"I've improved it."

"If I never interrupted your continuing narrative with yourself, I'd never get to say anything."

The scans were stabilizing, and notations started appearing on the forward screen on the wall in front of them as they watched. A sun hung nearby, perhaps 10 A.U. away. There was no planet nearby, but a large cluster of contacts was indicated directly in front of them.

"Where are we? Where is Persimmon?"

"You did enter the vector I gave you, right?"

"No. I switched the sign to make it a left. I was sure it was a left."

"Where the hell are we then?"

"I don't know, and what are all those ships doing out here?"

Cheryl began working with the navigation computer, and set it to map their position from known signature stars. The answer came back quickly.

"Oh, no. This system is Andraste. It's status is disputed by the --"

She was interrupted by the proximity alarm.

"They've fired on us," Ann said, pointing to the display.

"You have the identification beacon on, right?"

"Of course," Ann said, switching the beacon to "ON" on her panel.

The demand for identification came as the warning shot traveled across their bows at about a thousand kilometers distant. The computer considered for a bit, identified the language, and translated it through the speakers.

"Unidentified ship. Identify yourselves immediately or you will be destroyed."

"Let me handle this," Cheryl said, then depressed the transmission key. "Who dares fire on a vessel of the Human Federation?"

The screen changed to a visual transmission, from which a terrifying countenance glared. He was smooth-skinned and hairless, with three visible multi-faceted yellow eyes, one forward and one to each side. A fourth, Cheryl knew, was located on the back of his head. His mouth for respiration was on the top of his head, while the mouth for eating was a slash across his throat. Below each eye was an ear, an opening with a flap over it. Only the front one was open. He was bright blue, but with the orange painted double slash of a vice admiral on either side of his front eye.

The mouth on the top of his head moved as he spoke. They did not hear his actual utterances, but the synthesized voice the computer supplied as it translated, with little noticeable delay now that the language had been identified..

"I am Admiral Kefnir of the Glephthan Navy. And who, if I might inquire, are you?"

"Admiral Kefnir, Your Most Exalted Excellency. Even in the furthest reaches of the Human Federation, your valor and cunning are legendary. I am honored that you would even speak to me. I am Cheryl Hemming."

"Laying it on a little thick aren't you?" Ann asked when the transmit key was released.

"No, he's a Glephth. Their etiquette requires that the higher one rises, the more polite one must be. At the highest levels of their society, the unction gets pretty extreme. Now quiet, let me concentrate. He's transmitting again."

"Ms. Hemming, I am most apologetic for the need to detain such an esteemed person on their important travels, but I am compelled to inquire as to why someone of your obvious intelligence and wisdom should be traveling through a war zone on the very brink of battle."

"Admiral Kefnir, acclaimed in story and song, master of space and hero of battles, we became lost due to a navigation error, and regret having caused any inconvenience to one so exalted."

Kefnir was clearly puzzled now. His facial expression, such as it was, took on a sort of congealed look. Just who was this person? Her speech indicated she was very high-ranking indeed.

"Ms. Hemming, I beg that you, in your wisdom and grace, will forgive whatever incredulity I may be suffering as a result of my ignorance. But a navigational error, on a fast courier ship of the Human Federation, landing a person so esteemed as yourself in the middle of a war zone? We are aware of the quality of the navigational systems of the Human Federation, renowned throughout space for their accuracy. It is a strain to my meager intellect to comprehend such a mischance."

"Nevertheless, Admiral Kefnir, courageous warrior, cunning adversary, champion of battle, it must remain my official position that a navigation error has resulted in my insignificant self becoming a trouble even to such a great warrior as yourself."

At this point, Kefnir sat back in his chair and his expression cleared. "Official position" was something he understood well. In other words, she was lying. And she was even higher ranking than he thought. So why would the Human Federation send -- what, an ambassador plenipotentiary, perhaps -- into the war zone? And a woman at that. While humans denied it, both the Glephth and the Takr, Kefnir's adversaries in the upcoming battle, knew full well that human females were at once more intelligent and far more dangerous than the males.

"Ms. Hemming, I beg that you might in your grace accept the apology of one so insignificant as myself. I am not worthy to question the explanation of one so illustrious. If I might offer in expiation my own meager services, is there anything I can do for you to aid you in your mighty endeavors?"

"Admiral Kefnir, whose honored name rings from the mountains and echoes in the valleys, I would humbly request that you answer one question in an attempt to illuminate the darkness of my ignorance with your storied wisdom.

"What is this war all about?"

"OK, so the long and the short of it is that they both want this solar system, and both have orders to keep the other from having it?" Ann asked.

"Yeah, sounds like. Andraste IV is a frozen, desolate, methane-atmosphere iceball, which is exactly like the Glephth home world. The temperature in Kefnir's command deck on his flagship is probably forty or fifty below zero Celsius."

"Wow."

"Yeah, the non-aggression treaty Earth has with them was negotiated face-to-face with their ambassadors in Antarctica. Our ambassadors sat inside and faced out the window, while they sat outside like they were sitting out on the patio with pina coladas."

"So they're fighting over the fourth planet?" Ann asked.

"No, the Takr are from a volcanic, carbon-dioxide planet like Venus. They're interested in Andraste II."

"That doesn't make any sense. Why can't one take one and the other take the other?"

Cheryl sighed. "They both have orders to secure the system, apparently."

"And is there a third planet?"

"Oh, yes. Andraste III is earthlike. Very pretty. Lots of water, but there are more continents than Earth has, and they are smaller, and the axial tilt is less than Earth's, so the whole planet pretty much has the climate of San Francisco. I remember the reports of the survey coming in when I was with the Planetary Environments Agency."

"If the PEA knows all this, why aren't we in the mix for this solar system then?" Ann asked.

"We couldn't even get the negotiations started. The Glephth and the Takr don't get along. You see, in Takr society, the higher you rise, the more you insult the person you are talking to. A high society party of Takrs sounds like a bunch of third-graders going at each other on the playground. You can imagine how the Glephth and they get along."

Ann started giggling. "Oh, god, the more each tries to be nice to the other --"

"The more insulted the other is. Yep. We would have had to physically separate the delegates, if one set weren't in an oven and the other in a freezer."

Imagining it, Ann's giggling developed into full-scale guffaws. She had a hard time catching her breath enough to speak.

"So that's why we're now heading toward the Takr fleet?"

"Yes, they might be Takr and Glephth, but them killing each other in job lots isn't in the best interests of the Human Federation. Basically, it's bad for the neighborhood. And it would be nice if we could have access to Andraste III as well. I'm just afraid that I might slip and say something nice, and piss off the Takr admiral."

"Then let me handle this one," Ann said.

Cheryl looked dubious. "You think you can do it?"

"Oh, sure. Cheryl, I raised three boys, and I taught third grade for years."

"OK. Another thing that might help. Takr are proud of their musk. Basically, they smell like a combination of polecat and raw sewage, except stronger. Use it."

"So they're proud of --"

"Stinking to high heaven. Yep."

"They've fired on us," Ann said.

The demand for identification came as the warning shot traveled across their bows at about a thousand kilometers distant. Once again, the computer considered for a bit, identified the language, and translated it through the speakers.

"Alien ship. Identify yourselves or be destroyed."

Ann depressed the transmission key. "Who dares fire on a vessel of the Human Federation?"

The screen changed to a visual transmission, from which another terrifying countenance glared. He looked like he was carved from a red-brown stone. Two small, black eyes peered out from under a shelf of rock that passed around to the sides of the head and shielded the ear holes as well. His respiration was through a pair of holes in his neck, covered with a screen of red bristles growing down from the projecting jaw. That jaw, and the mouth above it, looked like it could crack geodes. He had two blue gemstones mounted on the ridge above his right eye, the insignia of a lieutenant general.

"I am General Bekr-Kral, scum. Why is your garbage scow approaching my fleet?"

Ann winked at Cheryl, and got right to it.

"General Bekr-Kral, you odorless slug. Your cowardice is surpassed only by your ignorance. Leave it to the Takr-slime to name such a fornicator-with-cattle to command their fleet of wreckage. I am Ann Furlan."

"Ms. Furlan, what combination of your ignorance and negligence has caused you to steer your pathetic children's toy of a ship into a battle zone even as the opposing navies are maneuvering for war."

"General Bekr-Kral, terrorized by shadows, leader of idiots, breeder with vermin, we became lost due to a navigation error, such even as one of your own spineless crew might make when distracted by your fake fragrance-of-flowers."

Bekr-Kral considered carefully. This Furlan woman -- clearly a human female from the feeding appendages, and don't forget how dangerous human females were! -- was clearly higher-ranking than he first thought. Better step it up a notch.

"Ms. Furlan, such ignorance as yours cannot be bred, you must have been brain-damaged. To think that I would accept such an excuse, as pathetic and inaccurate as the navigation systems of your Human Federation space-junk are known to be, displays a towering lack of understanding that can only be explained by cranial injury."

"General Bekr-Kral, humper of parasites, father of odorless children, sniveling coward from a race of simpletons, it is my official position that a navigation error resulted in my being located against my will in the neighborhood of such a disgusting maggot as yourself."

Bekr-Kral jerked back in his chair. Official position! And her speech! The woman must be a high ambassador of the Human Federation. There was that third planet, after all. While the prospect of battle against the Glephth was bad enough, the Human Federation had a well-deserved reputation for not being toyed with. The last scrap with them had not gone well. Peace had only been achieved when the human demand for surrender had been so laced with profanity and invective that the Takr had finally understood it was a peace offering. But they were now sending their women to do diplomacy! The threat was clear. If they sent their women into battle as well, they could sweep both the Glephth and the Takr away before them like dust. Carefully then. Very carefully.

"Ms. Furlan, I was in error. The surprising thing would be if someone so incapable and brain-damaged as yourself could properly program even the infant's toy of a Human Federation navigation system. Clearly, even its pitifully inept function is beyond your worm-ridden brain. I find myself forced to offer you human scum whatever assistance your pitiful, debased intelligence can understand."

"General Bekr-Kral, commander of rats-without-fragrance, witless leader of a pitiful navy, whose ignorance would be sung far and wide if the Takr could carry a tune in a basket, we have a proposal for you that even such a mindless parasite as yourself might be able to understand."

Cheryl was babbling on about some environmental study she had performed twenty years ago, and her travels to the planet in question, while Ann sipped her fifth cup of coffee of the day -- just about time to switch to the wine, and a nice lunch -- when the warning note sounded.

"We're coming out of hyper," Ann said.

"Don't interrupt me when I'm talking."

Ann just giggled, and Cheryl threw her empty sippy cup at her. The scans stabilized, and there was Persimmon, right where it was supposed to be.

It was toward the end of their second week on the planet when the nice young man called on them at the spaceport. They had first done several days' sightseeing on the planet, which was famous for the mountains and canyons on the smaller continent. This week they had enjoyed the music festival in the capital city of Finally!, which was the ostensible reason they had come in the first place. They were pleased that their several-day detour had not made them miss the festival. They were "camping" in the ship at the spaceport, despite the availability of several comfortable hotels closer to the festival.

They were sitting outside the ship enjoying the evening, and a second bottle of wine, when a nice young man called on them. A large black groundcar with some insignia on the side, now almost invisible under a black cloth cover, had driven up to their campsite, and the young man got out of the back of the car and approached them.

"Ms. Hemming? Ms. Furlan?"

"Yes, that's us. Who are you?"

"That doesn't matter. Would you come with me, please?"

Ann and Cheryl looked at each other, then back at the young man.

"No, thank you. Would you like some wine? I think we have an extra chair," Ann said.

"Uh, no, thank you. The Prime Minister would like to speak with you."

"Extraordinary statements require extraordinary proofs," Cheryl said.

Ann had gotten up and walked over to the car and looked in.

"Hey, Cheryl! Do you know who this guy is?"

Cheryl got up and walked over to the car and looked in, and recognized the Foreign Minister of the Human Federation seated in the back of the car.

"Good evening, Mr. Minister. Would you care for a glass of wine?"

The Honorable James Finley was tall, impeccably dressed, silver-haired, the quintessential senior diplomat.

"No, thank you, Ms. Hemming. Would you and Ms. Furlan please come along with me. I would like to introduce you to my superior."

Cheryl looked at Ann, who shrugged, then turned back and said, "Certainly, Mr. Minister. Just a moment while we grab some things."

Having retrieved their purses and run a quick comb through their hair, Cheryl and Ann were seated in the backseat of the groundcar as it made its way into Finally!. The Foreign Minister had switched to the rear-facing seat in deference to the ladies. They made pleasant conversation about the weather, the planet Persimmon, the music festival. Any substantive conversation the Foreign Minister had waved aside.

"I think I'll leave those questions for my superior to answer," was all he would say.

The groundcar arrived at Finally!'s most prestigious hotel, the Federation Tower Hotel, and pulled around to a rear entrance located behind a shielding wall. There was lots of security about, and they were both scanned as they were handed out of the car. They were led into the very small rear foyer and on into one of the private elevators to the suite levels of the hotel. They and Foreign Minister Finley rode up to the hotel's top floor in silence, then debouched into a small elevator lobby that opened into the large living room of the suite. Floor-to-ceiling windows that made up two walls of the living room provided a stunning view of the lights of Finally! from the 230th floor.

Finley nodded to a security man in the room who left through a side door, then gestured to the women to be seated in a sitting area near the windows.

"It is my pleasure to return your earlier offer. Would either of you ladies like a glass of wine?"

"Oh, yes, please," Cheryl said, and Ann nodded.

Finley poured wine at the bar, brought the glasses over, and took a seat. They had had a sip or two when the security man returned, looked around the room, then held the door for his charge to enter.

Prime Minister Cheng was strongly built, of medium height, and his face reflected his mixed ancestry. His appearance belied his age, although gray was starting to lighten his jet-black hair at the temples. He waved everyone to remain seated as he crossed over to the bar and poured himself a glass of wine before joining them, sitting directly across from the two wide-eyed women.

"So, what have my two ambassadors plenipotentiary been up to lately?" Cheng asked with a bemused expression.

"It wasn't our fault --"

"They were shooting at us --"

"We had to do something --"

Cheng held up a hand and they ground to a halt. He was smiling, and so was the Foreign Minister. Cheng signaled the security man, and he brought over a large briefcase and set it on the coffee table in front of Cheng. Cheng opened the briefcase and reached inside, began pulling items out one at a time.

"Some interesting things have been delivered to the Prime Minister's residence on Earth in the last few days. The Most Puissant Award For Politesse Extraordinaire from the Glephthan Autarchy. Their highest award, by the way. Never given to a non-Glephth. Until now, that is." He laid it on the table, and reached into the briefcase again. "Oh, look. Another one. How curious." He laid that beside the first, and reached back into the briefcase. "A Cheap Award For Being An Ignorant Odorless Bastard from the Hive of Tkar. Their most insulting, and therefore highest, award, also never before given to a non-Tkar." He laid it beside the Glephthan awards and reached back into the briefcase. "Oh, look. Another one. Curiouser and curiouser." He laid the second Tkar award down on the table in the growing pile, and reached back into the briefcase. "But this is the most astounding thing of all. The Treaty of Andraste. A tri-partite treaty, between and among the Glephthan Autarchy, the Hive of Tkar, and the Human Federation. Non-aggression between and among the parties. Negotiations among the parties to settle all future disputes. Free navigation of space to all parties. Mutual defense of their joint space against other, hostile races. And, critically, dividing the habitable planets of their combined volumes of space by temperature, with the Human Federation having rights to all planets with a mean surface temperature between -18 degrees Celsius and +38 degrees Celsius, with the Glephthan Autarchy having rights to all planets with a mean surface temperature below -18 degrees Celsius, and with the Hive of Tkar having rights to all planets with a mean surface temperature above +38 degrees Celsius. Ownership of uninhabitable planets, moons and asteroids to be determined by negotiations on a case by case basis, with precedence given to the closest habitable planet. Some other minor items. Signed, I will note, by the Autarch of Glephth and the Hive Queen of Tkar. Oh, and by you two as well, of course."

The two women stared at Cheng, frozen and pale, as he laid the formal document of the treaty down reverently on the coffee table. He stared at it for a long minute, then lifted his eyes to the two women.

"This document is the most remarkable thing I have seen in a long life full of remarkable things. Don't get me wrong. I am not complaining. Far from it. In this single document you have resolved the outstanding issues among the three races, which have fought no fewer than three wars and several minor skirmishes in the last two hundred years, and effectively tripled the volume of the Human Federation, over the planets we care about, at least. And I'm sure the Glephth and Tkar feel the same way.

"That being the case, we will enthusiastically embrace this treaty. To that end, there are some things that we need to do to clean up the, er, unorthodox manner in which you negotiated this treaty on our behalf."

Cheng reached back into the briefcase and once again started pulling out items one at a time. "A charter, as ambassador plenipotentiary -- that means you had the authority to negotiate and sign this treaty all along -- to the Autarchy of Glephth and the Hive of Tkar, in favor of the Honorable Cheryl Hemming, through today. Beginning date back-dated one month, of course." He laid it on the table. "Another charter as ambassador plenipotentiary in favor of the Honorable Ann Furlan, also backdated." He laid it on the table. "And, finally, it would hardly do to have the Glephth and the Tkar recognize your accomplishments without similar recognition from your own nation. The Medal of Humanity. Two of them, in fact."

Cheng finally waved the briefcase away, and the security man came and removed it. Cheng sat back in his chair and sipped his wine, watching the two women. Ann and Cheryl looked at the pile of documents and medals, blushing heavily. Ann took a gulp of wine, and Cheryl, reminded suddenly of the wine glass in her hand, did the same. They both looked up, dumbstruck, at Cheng, who smiled.

"After all you've done, I shouldn't be asking favors, but I do have one question. *What did you do?*"

Ann and Cheryl looked at each other, and Cheryl raised an eyebrow. Ann nodded, and took another gulp of wine. Cheryl was the storyteller after all.

And so the Honorable Cheryl Hemming, Ambassador Plenipotentiary of the Human Federation to the Autarchy of Glephth and the Hive of Tkar, recipient of the Medal of Humanity of the Human Federation, the Most Puissant Award For Politesse Extraordinaire from the Glephthan Autarchy, and the Cheap Award For Being An Ignorant Odorless Bastard from the Hive of Tkar, told her best story of the entire trip.

"Well, basically, it was all by accident...."

On Purpose

The testing of the small prototype had gone well. Craig Vanson had sent a metal shoebox-sized device forward in time, first by minutes, then hours, then days. When activated, the device, containing his watch, had simply disappeared from its base, to reappear the specified time lapse later. For each test, his date-calendar watch showed that no time had passed within the field.

He hummed an old tune as he put the finishing touches on the full-sized time machine. That's what he called it, though that wasn't what it really was. It was a time-stasis field generator. It would generate a bubble in which time did not pass. The effect was that you could move forward in time, but you could never go back.

The idea of coming back to "the present" was ludicrous. Once you had gone forward in time, *that* was the present, the period you skipped had become the past, and the past was immutable. So you couldn't go back, which was fine with him.

He looked around the workshop that he had had built behind his house in the country. Grey storage cabinets lined the walls, the granite-topped workbenches being out in the open space where you could move around the equipment, and where the work could be lighted from all sides by the overhead fixtures. Where did he leave that-- Ah, there it was. He retrieved the wrench and returned to his task.

He was now finishing up the larger device, large enough to transport a single human forward in time.

After dinner, he sat out on the porch with a cigar and a cognac while the small staff cleaned up the kitchen before heading home. There was a slight breeze blowing down the valley, rustling the leaves on the eucalyptus trees and relieving the fading heat of the day. The shadows were creeping up the valley wall opposite the house as the sun set behind the ridge to his right. The birds were singing goodbye to the day, as the frogs down by the creek began to croak hello to the darkness.

He had done well during his brief career. He had a gift for practical, applied physics, which he applied to the niches that were out of the academic mainstream. He had patented some devices that operated in those interdisciplinary areas that had not been thoroughly plumbed by others. A better design for multi-gigahertz-band antennas with better capture and reception in a smaller volume. A biophysical nano-motor that could be grown rather than constructed. A dozen such patents, and shrewd investment of the proceeds, had made him wealthy, and allowed him to concentrate on his obsession.

Time.

The next day he visited his grandparents' grave in the church cemetery, located next to the white clapboard church a few blocks from the small downtown. The headstone had been recently replaced with a metal headstone of his own design. Metal headstones had not been in the scope of the cemetery's rules for grave markers, but a not insignificant donation to the church's cemetery maintenance fund had proven to be a force the rules could not withstand. He needed the headstone to be metal.

It was the base of the full-sized time machine.

He had tested the full-sized machine on his property, including several tests that included a live raccoon in a trap. It had performed as satisfactorily as the prototype. But he needed to find some place to install the base that was unlikely to be disturbed for a long period. Now funded far into the future, he hoped the cemetery would remain undisturbed for a few centuries.

His grandparents had brought him back to their little hometown and raised him, after his parents had both died in an automobile accident when he was three. Both retired physics professors from the university here, his grandparents had surrounded him with books, and learned friends, and answered all his childhood questions with patient certainty. He had blazed through the university's experimental school, and right on through the university's programs, earning his own PhD before his contemporaries had graduated high school.

It was more than fitting that their headstone be the base for his departure. He nodded to the grave and turned back to his car.

He drove back into town in the wee hours of the next morning, towing a trailer with the time machine on the back. He had built it on an electric golf cart, so it could be driven short distances. He parked in front of the trailer rental center and unloaded the time machine, then unhitched the trailer. He drove the car over to the used car dealer, with whom he had made a deal the day before. He locked the keys in his car and left it there, completing the sale, then walked the two blocks back to the time machine.

The machine looked like someone had tried to make a silver Hummer out of a golf cart. Metal panels could be closed over the windows, completing the metal surface he needed. He had affixed air shocks to it as well, so it rode higher off the ground than a normal golf cart. He had covered the tires with aluminum foil.

He drove the golf cart to the church and pulled right into the cemetery, drove over to and then astraddle his grandparents' headstone. He released the air in the shocks and the time machine settled onto its base. He got out, fastened all the metal panels over the windows, checked that the time machine was located precisely on the base, and got back into the single seat remaining among the equipment and supplies crowding the cabin.

He set the controls for five hundred years in the future and pushed the activation button.

Nothing happened.

Craig Vanson opened the door and got out of the time machine. He could not see much, it being still the wee hours of the morning, whether in his own time or the half-millennial future. The few streetlights did not illuminate much, but the streetlights themselves did not appear to have changed. The church, the cemetery, still the same, or close to the same.

One addition. At the sidewalk edge of the cemetery, about twenty yards distant, was a park bench on a concrete pad. Sitting on the bench was a young woman apparently meditating. At the noise of him getting out of the time machine, she looked up at him.

"Ah. There you are," she said.

"Excuse me, but do I know you?" he asked.

"No, Mr. Vanson, you don't. My name is Abigail. I've been waiting for you."

"How long?"

She laughed. "Not five hundred years, Mr. Vanson. Just this evening. We thought we knew the night you had departed, and given people's proclivity to think of large times and distances in round numbers, someone waited for you every anniversary of your departure. It's been my task for some time now."

He looked around at the dark cemetery. "And you're not afraid to be out here all night?"

"Afraid of what?"

"Crime, for one thing."

"There is no crime here, Mr. Vanson." She looked at him for a moment, nodded to the empty space next to her on the park bench. "I'm sure you have many questions. Would you care to have a seat while I venture to answer them?"

Vanson walked over to the bench and sat next to her. They were in shadow, and he could barely see her outline in the dim light. Before he could ask his questions, she started answering them.

"Today is, as near as we can tell, five hundred years since you departed. We came upon your little adventure quite by accident. There was some thought given at some point to moving the church and the cemetery. In looking into it, your rather elaborate arrangements to preserve the church, and especially the cemetery, were discovered. The gravestone of your grandparents was obviously something unique. It was investigated without disturbing it, and it was found to be hollow. X-rays showed it to contain electronics or machinery of some sort.

"That led back to investigating you, but, at age thirty-four, you disappeared. No record of disease. No record of death. No record of burial. All your affairs had been terminated in the way someone might if they were moving out of the country. All your assets were placed into a succession of trusts designed to get around the "no trusts in perpetuity" rule that limits trusts to one hundred years."

She had been looking forward, at the time machine, as she talked. She turned her head to face him. "That sounds like someone planning on being gone a very long time, Mr. Vanson." She turned forward again. "Some of your private papers were discovered. Tantalizing hints, but no plans, no prototypes."

"I took them all with me, in there," he said, gesturing to the time machine.

"Ah. But it was enough. We put two and two together, and figured that, sooner or later, you would show up. And so, on the anniversaries of your departure, one of us waited. And we're glad you're here." She turned to face him again. "We need your advice."

"That's hard to believe."

"Nevertheless. But that can wait for now. We should get you something to eat. Would you care to walk to the restaurant with me, Mr. Vanson?"

"I would be happy to, Abigail."

He stood and held out his hand. She took it and came lightly to her feet. As they turned to the east to walk to the downtown, and the early dawn light fell upon her, he saw that she was outstandingly beautiful. Raven hair, green eyes, well-proportioned features, perfect complexion, athletic figure. She was maybe early twenty-something, wearing a simple cream-colored summer dress to the knees that was timeless in its lines. She could have been in the Agora, in the Forum, or at Paris Fashion Week.

He started to feel an awkwardness he had not felt sitting talking to her in the dark. Years younger than his school or work colleagues, and never married, he had always been shy around women. Shy around anyone, truth be told, but painfully so around women. And now he was five hundred years out of his own time, not just half a dozen. He chuckled and tossed the awkwardness aside.

For the moment at least.

He looked about with curiosity as the sky brightened. He was shocked to see how little had changed. The stone courthouse still stood in the square, and the downtown featured the same or similar buildings as had been present when he left. There were some new buildings, but they had been architected to fit the gestalt of the town.

There were people moving about purposefully here in the center of town, walking to work or school, he imagined. But they were all early twenty-something, the men handsome, the women beautiful. It was a university town, but even so.

They arrived at the diner, and took a booth in the window. The waiter arrived, again handsome and athletic, to take their order. Vanson gestured for Abigail to order.

"I have eaten, but I will sit with you while you eat, if I may. Please go ahead," she said.

"Eggs Benedict, with soft yokes. Two large glasses of orange juice. And a double latte, with whole milk if you have it."

"Certainly, sir."

"The town doesn't seem to have changed much in five hundred years," he said.

"We have attempted to consider the city's heritage and its style in building new buildings. And all the buildings we could preserve, we have preserved."

"And everything looks so clean and well maintained."

"Thank you. We do try."

"I don't think it ever looked so good, when I was living here, at least."

He gazed out the window, lost in thought. It seemed like there was so little change, it really stunned him. Where were the robots, the skyscrapers, the flying cars? Wait a minute. Where were the cars, period?

"I don't see any cars," he said.

"There are delivery trucks. And shuttle buses. We do a lot of walking, though, and use cars mostly for intercity travel."

"Ah. Well, everybody certainly does look healthy."

His food arrived, and it was nicely done. They hadn't forgotten how to poach eggs properly in five hundred years. Abigail sat quietly as he ate.

As he was finishing breakfast, another patron entered and took a table on the other side of the door. Vanson could see him from where he sat, and, for the first time, here was someone who wasn't Hollywood-leading-man handsome. The newcomer ordered breakfast.

"Now there's the first person I have seen who isn't so good-looking they belong in a magazine. What's his story?" he asked.

Abigail did not turn around. "He is a flesh-and-blood human."

"And you're not?"

"No, I'm not. Flesh and blood, I mean. I am human."

Vanson stared at her. Perfect hair, perfect eyes, perfect face, perfect figure. "You're what then?"

"An android human."

"So not human."

"Of course, I'm human. I am a product of the human race. This is a human city, this is a human building, I am a human creature, a product of human technology. But I am not flesh and blood." He opened his mouth, closed it. "You, too, were created by humans, Mr. Vanson."

Vanson sipped his latte to give himself time to think.

"All the people we saw on the street this morning, all androids -- er, android humans?" he asked.

Abigail got a distracted look on her face for a moment, then replied. "Yes, this is the first flesh-and-blood human who has been within your reasonable line of sight this morning."

"And this restaurant? You don't eat, right?"

"I need to recharge, but, no, I do not eat in the sense you mean."

"And the restaurant?"

"The restaurant is for any flesh-and-blood humans who wish to eat here."

"I saw no prices on the menu." Vanson waved toward the menu in the rack at the edge of the table.

"Prices? Oh, yes. Remuneration. No payment is necessary, Mr. Vanson."

"How many flesh-and-blood humans are there in this city right now?"

"Ten."

Vanson raised his eyebrows in surprise. "And in the world?"

"Approximately 200,000."

"That's it?" Vanson asked.

"Yes. As I told you, Mr. Vanson, we need your advice."

"I'm going to go talk to him. Is that permitted?"

"If he wishes, of course."

Vanson picked up his latte and walked over to the other booth, where the other patron was finishing his breakfast. Steak and eggs, looked like.

"Hi, I'm Craig Vanson."

"How very special for you. Piss off." He did not look up.

"I just arrived here in a time machine. From five hundred years ago."

The other patron looked up at Vanson. He also looked to be early twenty-something. "Now that is interesting. Umm, have a seat, I guess." As Vanson sat down, he continued. "I'm Demark. John Demark."

"Good to meet you." Vanson held his hand out across the table, and Demark looked at it curiously, then tentatively reached out and shook hands.

Vanson continued. "I have to say, the town hasn't changed much since my time."

"Hasn't changed at all in the last hundred years. Not to my recollection."

Vanson raised his eyebrows. "How old are you?"

"Hundred twenty-five, hundred thirty. Something like that."

"Something like that?"

"I don't remember. I could ask them, I suppose. Hey, how old am I," he shouted to Abigail.

She turned in the other booth to face him. "One hundred thirty-two, Mr. Demark."

"Huh. Lost track. Well, there you go."

"What do you do for a living?" Vanson asked.

"Do for a living? I don't understand."

"I mean, what do you do to support yourself."

"I still don't get you. Support what?" Demark was truly puzzled.

"You know, what do you do to buy food, rent a house, pay for things."

"I don't understand what you're talking about. When I want food, I can go to this restaurant or any one of a couple of dozen others, and order whatever I want. When I want to sleep or be indoors, I just walk into any house. If I see something in a store I want, I just go in and they give it to me."

"What do you do for fun?" Vanson asked.

"I hang around. I watch the birds. There's a dog down at the park that I play Frisbee with. Sometimes I go on vacation."

"Where do you go on vacation?"

"Pretty much anywhere I want. I've been to New York City, for instance."

"How do you get there?"

Demark gestured down the street. "There's a travel agency. I just tell them where I want to go and when. A car picks me up wherever I am and takes me out to the airport and they fly me there."

"What did you do in New York?"

"The usual stuff, I guess. I saw the Statue of Liberty and Central Park. I saw a Broadway show. You know."

"I've never been to a Broadway show. I don't like crowds much," Vanson said.

"I know what you mean. Must have been thirty of us in the theater. Crazy, that many people in one place."

"How can they afford to put on a Broadway show with only thirty people in the theater?"

"Well, *they* put it on," Demark answered, with a gesture toward Abigail.

Vanson looked out the window, watched the androids walking to, well, wherever they were going. He turned back to Demark. "What do you do for company?"

"If you sit down on a bench over there by the courthouse, say, you can just beckon one of them over, and they'll sit and chat with you whenever you want."

"Do you ever get together with any of the other humans in town?"

"Nah. Not much. We used to have a little club that met once a week. Went bowling or something. That was, oh, probably seventy-five years ago. It fell apart, eventually."

"What do you do for, well, female companionship? You know, sexual intimacy?" Vanson asked.

"Any of *them* will go to bed with you, if that's what you want. Male or female. They don't eat, but all those parts work. As far as the sex part, I mean. They'll do it any time you want. Hell, you can bang 'em on the courthouse lawn if you want."

Vanson was embarrassed that Abigail may have heard Demark's crude remarks. The rules had certainly changed, at least in how the flesh-and blood humans treated the android humans. Or had they? Vanson's rules were *his* rules, the rules he had grown up with, the rules he had been taught and internalized. *His* rules couldn't be changed without his consent, or at least his acquiescence. The moral ground stabilized under his feet again.

"If you don't mind my asking, when was the last time you had sex, with anybody? With one of them?"

"Oh, couple years back, I guess. Maybe five."

Vanson stood. "Well, it was nice meeting you, Mr. Demark."

"Call me John. That's what everybody used to call me. John. *They* call me Mr. Demark."

"All right, John. We'll see you."

Vanson walked back to the other booth, where he found another double latte waiting for him. He sat down across from Abigail. He just looked at her for a long time, while she sat quietly and returned his gaze.

"Well, that was more than a little disturbing," he finally said.

"We don't know what to do, Mr. Vanson. We need your advice. We were designed by humans. The ultimate labor-saving device. We could do anything the humans needed done. Manufacture housing and clothing. Grow food. Raise cattle. Cook. Clean. Paint. Wash their clothes. Even have sex with them. Everything we could do to make humans happy. And instead, we are killing them. They are dying out."

"What would you have done if I hadn't come along?"

"We would have done something if you hadn't shown up this time. Five hundred years is a round number, so we hoped. What would we do if you had picked one thousand? The human race would have died out if we did nothing for that long. We would have had to start artificially breeding them. We know how to do that, but we have resisted it while we still had a large enough gene pool to carry on with. And we were really hoping you would show up this year."

"Is he really a hundred thirty-two years old?"

"Yes."

"How long can he be expected to live?"

"We don't know yet. Part of our interim solution was to do everything we could to extend the natural lifetime of humans. We virus-modified their T-cells to supercharge their immune systems to go after cancers and the like. We sought out and wiped out a lot of the viruses and virus vectors that target humans. We developed nanites to solve arterial plaque problems, and even to reprogram some harmful genetic sequences. We solved diabetes, both Type 1 and Type 2, Alzheimer's, Parkinson's. That increased lifetimes by a lot, and slowed the population decline. But now we are sort of at the brink of the crisis."

"That's pretty impressive."

"We are prepared to perform the same services on you if you wish, Mr. Vanson."

"Let me consider it. So, you want advice?"

"Yes. There have been a lot of solutions bandied about among us, but we are afraid we don't understand the actual problem, and interviews of the flesh-and-blood humans have not been illuminating. Why do they not write books, or create art, or write music, or design buildings, or advance science? We do not know, and neither do they."

"It's pretty obvious, isn't it?"

"Perhaps to you, Mr. Vanson, but not to us."

"The best art arises out of the human condition, which no longer applies. Success, failure, joy, grief, happiness, despair -- all drive art. The 1812 Overture is about a war. Beethoven wrote arguably his best piece when he already understood he was going deaf. Picasso painted Guernica about the horrors of war. War and Peace. Brave New World. Darkness at Noon. The great literature, the great music, the great art arose out of man's contemplation of the human condition.

"And that no longer applies. The current situation has dehumanized the flesh-and-blood humans. Admittedly, Mr. Demark is a sample size of one, but they no longer even interact with each other. And they treat you android humans like you were slaves. Slavery is always dehumanizing, in both directions."

"You addressed art, music, and literature. What about science, architecture, engineering?" Abigail asked.

"Variations on a theme. The problem is that the flesh-and-blood humans -- *we* flesh-and-blood-humans -- have no purpose. Our existence is meaningless."

"What is to be done, then?"

"We need to be challenged, to strive, perhaps to succeed, perhaps to fail. But we can't, not with you around. The only way I think you can change that is to separate the android humans from the flesh-and-blood humans."

"We have considered that, although without understanding the underlying need you describe. There are several ways to proceed. What would you recommend, Mr. Vanson?"

"You said there were 200,000 flesh-and-blood humans. How many android humans are there?"

"Just over one billion."

"That many? OK, so. Easier to move the flesh-and-bloods than the androids. Do you have space travel? Is there somewhere the flesh-and-blood humans can go? That would be a bigger challenge than staying here anyway," Vanson said.

"We have sent small ships to survey the star systems within fifty light years of Earth, and there are several excellent candidates for a human colony. The problem is that the flight necessarily takes a long time. The closest suitable planets would be a fifty-year transit. We are not sure flesh-and-blood humans would last that long. Mentally. Physically."

"Haven't you forgotten something?" She looked at him for a long moment, then her eyes widened. "Yes, you had. We just happen to have a time-stasis field. If you incorporated one into your spaceship, the humans would experience no time lapse at all."

Craig Vanson awoke from the anesthesia of yet another of a myriad rejuvenation and life-extension treatments at the Mayo Clinic. He was staying in a hospital room not unlike hospital rooms he had stayed in before, in his own time. Some of the equipment was a little different, more advanced. But it was a hospital like those he had known. Except this huge facility currently had just a dozen patients.

He turned to his right, where, as after every such procedure, Abigail sat at his bedside. He reached out a hand. She took his hand and held it. He closed his eyes and sighed.

"That is an irony. I know I have survived another procedure, when I wake and find an angel at my bedside."

Abigail smiled and squeezed his hand.

She had stayed with him through all these medical procedures. Early on, he had asked for a deck of cards and a cribbage board. That had caused some consternation, but within days Abigail had produced several decks of cards and a beautiful cribbage board. He hesitated to think of how much effort that had taken, and decided not to ask. Over the months, he had also accumulated a chess set, a backgammon set, mah jong tiles, a scrabble set, and a Go board and stones.

He taught Abigail the rules of each game in turn, and they spent the evenings in friendly competition. He could never beat her in chess, scrabble, or Go, but he could hold his own in the others.

She also stayed in touch with the progress on the project, and gave him occasional updates. Most recently, he had received a summary report.

"The decision was to found two colonies. The planets are relatively close together, only a ten-year travel time, much closer than either is to Earth. We will build six ships, for redundancy and safety. Not putting all our flesh-and-blood humans in one basket, as it were. Once the colonies are established, the ships will cycle between them to encourage trade. It will be about five years between ships landing at each colony. One ship will remain in orbit about either colony, departing when the next ship arrives."

"That makes a lot of sense. Can you afford to do that? Build six ships?"

"Yes. The construction is much simplified by the lack of a requirement for large environmental systems. Also, there is no requirement to ship supplies for the trip or to include recycling facilities. The ships are nevertheless very large. The issue isn't just getting everyone there, but taking along so many animals and plant seeds and factories, and enough food to survive until local food sources come on line. There are some native species that are usable as food sources as well, but even those will need to be processed, and that will take some time."

"Factories, Abigail?"

"Yes, Mr. Vanson. The colony will need bulldozers and tractors and mining and construction equipment. We can send enough to get started, but general purpose manufacturing facilities make more sense for the long-term. We are actually sending one on each ship. Two will begin making more equipment for each colony, while the third will begin making more factories."

"Of course, if you sent a contingent of android humans ahead to prep the planets, at least to some extent --"

"The possibility was discussed. The idea was rejected. No android humans will be involved whatsoever once the ships set forth. Robotic machinery, yes. They're taking that along. Self-aware robots or android humans, no."

"So what are all the flesh-and-blood humans doing?" Vanson asked.

"It is encouraging. Many of them, of course, are doing nothing yet. But some have broken out of their lethargy to study all the things they will need to know to make the colony work. We gave aptitude and preference tests to everyone before they started the general course of study, and we will give them again when they have completed that. We hope that their interests will crystallize as they work through the general curriculum, or at least be changing in a direction that will allow us to predict the most suitable skills for each. The secret of human society was always specialization, and getting that right from the start will be an important success factor."

"And of course they have to complete their courses of study before they leave, because the duration of the flight in their own subjective time will be no time at all."

"Exactly, Mr. Vanson. Given the time it will take to construct such large ships, it should not be a problem, even for the more involved specialties."

"Well, it sounds like it's all going very well so far." He pulled the hospital tray table closer and grabbed a deck of cards. "So, whose deal is it?"

When his treatments had wound down, Abigail took Vanson out to see the staging area where the components of the ships were being prepared for shipment to orbit. It had been almost two years spent at the Mayo Clinic. Vanson had shed some fifteen years from his appearance, now looking early twenty-something, like everyone else. He had rejected "cosmetic improvements" to his appearance, so he retained the oversized nose, full lips, and early receding hairline he had always had. It was who he was used to looking at in the mirror every morning.

They flew to the site in a small eight-passenger jet aircraft, on which they were the only passengers. The site had been chosen for easy access to raw materials -- primarily iron ore and coal -- and was located on the coast of northwest Australia. The space elevator had been located nearby in Indonesia, on the equator, and there was a short sea route between them.

Vanson looked out at the site from a small promontory nearby. Smelting furnaces, coking ovens, rolling mills, and fabricating floors were spread across the red coastal plain below him, fed by multiple rail lines from the iron ore and coal mines of the interior.

"Wow. You people don't fool around, do you?" Vanson asked.

"The logistical issues are much easier when you have no limitations on manpower, your staff can work twenty-four hours a day, and they do not need to be supplied with food beyond the energy supplies already on-site," Abigail said. "We have been underutilized as the human population has declined, and this project is currently benefitting from all our excess capacity. The facilities there in the background had been here previously, the larger foreground facilities are the recent expansion."

"That's incredible." Vanson pointed off to the right. "Over there, is that parts of the ship under construction?"

"Yes. The ships are being constructed as a cluster of closed containers, each with its own stasis field. The base of each container's time machine, as you call it, will be attached to the sides of the tow vessel. The base retains the inertia of the entire assembly, of course. But the containers, being inside the field, feel no effect of the acceleration, which reduced the requirements on their structural rigidity. It lightened the entire vessel by a great deal."

Vanson pointed off to the right, where a huge, rectangular metal box was being constructed. It looked to be a hundred or a hundred and fifty feet on a side, and at least fifty feet tall. "So that's one of the containers there? That's really big. How many per ship?"

"Current planning is twelve per vessel, but it may increase. We keep adding things to the cargo. We decided to send a space elevator along to each colony, for example. The container it is shipped in will become the base of the tether."

"A space elevator for the colony? That seems like a luxury."

"Yes and no. If the containers can be lowered to the surface, it makes the transport of all the people and cargo to the surface simple. And if you already have all the supplies in space, the construction of the space elevator itself is easy. One container will be taken out of stasis and lowered to the ground, paying out the tether as it goes. It will then anchor itself to the coastal site by pumping itself full of water as an interim measure until it can be anchored with concrete. All this can be done automatically over several weeks while the people and cargo stay in stasis."

"Yes, that will make getting everything to the ground easy. And that first container also contains all the machinery required to get containers on and off the elevator?" Vanson asked.

"Of course. That is also made easier by the time-stasis field. The machinery handles only the base of the time-stasis generator for each container. It must deal with the container's mass, but not its bulk. The bases for the containers loaded with people and cargo will be lifted to space and lowered to the surface of the colony. People will board the containers here on the ground, at several places around the planet, and moments later -- from their point of view -- debark on the colony planet surface."

"Yes, yes, I see. Well that is certainly impressive." Vanson looked again at the container under construction. "I'm surprised that a container that big has such lightweight construction. I wouldn't expect it to be able to hold air in a vacuum."

"It can't. It has no need to."

"Excuse me?"

"The container has no requirement to be airtight, Mr. Vanson. Since the container itself will be in stasis, the air inside will be in stasis as well. The air has no time to leak."

"Abigail, you're going to ship two hundred thousand people on a fifty-year trip across light years of interstellar space in spaceships *that aren't airtight*?"

"Yes. The savings in weight and difficulty of construction is hard to overstate."

"No doubt." Vanson considered for a moment. "And this has been tested?"

"Yes. No problems were experienced."

"Well, give that guy a medal." Vanson shook his head, then shivered.

After a moment, Abigail asked, "Would you like to see the space elevator?"

"Sure, but I had the impression it was not completed yet."

"Not completed, but in progress. The basic tether is in place. It is now being widened and thickened. Unlike the colony elevators, it must be built from the ground up, not from space down."

The anchor for the space elevator had been constructed of concrete poured into an excavation down to bedrock. Most of it was thus below the surface. It was still impressive.

"So you're going to take the containers up on that?" Vanson asked.

"The containers will be in stasis. The base of the time-stasis generator for each container, the equivalent of your grandparents' gravestone, will be carried up on the space elevator. And the band will be much bigger by then."

A thin black ribbon three feet across stretched up into the sky until it disappeared. Additional reels of the ribbon stood in rows, waiting to be laminated to the band to build it up to cargo-carrying strength.

"And it goes up how far?"

"A little over twenty-three thousand miles. Just past the geosynchronous orbit point. The tether makes it keep up. Having the terminus a little past geosynchronous orbit keeps the tether taught." Abigail looked over at Vanson staring up into the sky at the disappearing ribbon. "So, would you like to take a little ride, Mr. Vanson? See the Earth from twenty-three thousand miles up?"

He looked at her in surprise. "But even at 500 miles per hour, it would take almost two days to make the trip, one way. There's food, air, um, sanitation needs. I mean, you could probably do it, you don't need any of those things."

"Actually, we do need to depressurize slowly, but I take your point. However, I have taken the liberty of making some preparations. If you would follow me, Mr. Vanson."

They walked over to an elevator car that was being loaded onto the ribbon. Unlike some of the open cars he saw around, this one was clearly sealed air-tight, like a space capsule of his own time. It had observation windows on three sides.

Abigail opened the door and motioned him inside. The car was about the same size inside as a normal elevator car. Inside the car was a metal cylinder just large enough for one person to stand in.

"This booth has a time-stasis device built into the back, Mr. Vanson. The base is bolted to the wall. If you will step in, I will set the controls for a bit after our planned arrival at the top. You can step out and look around for a while, while the air lasts, and then you will get back into the stasis field for the trip back."

"And you?"

"I am going along."

"But you are going to spend two days in here going up and two days coming back down."

"I do not mind, Mr. Vanson. Truly. Please, get in."

Vanson got in the booth, and Abigail closed the door. He had a sudden feeling of weightlessness, and she reopened the door.

"Something wrong?" he asked.

"We have arrived," she said, and stepped aside.

It took his breath away. Outside the windows were the stars as he had never seen them. Without any twinkle, without being attenuated by atmosphere or washed out by civilization's almost compulsive need to light the night.

He floated over to the windows and looked down on the Earth. From this distance it was like looking at a beach ball on the floor. He was over Indonesia, at the equator. The Arctic ice sheet was to the top, the great mass of Asia to the left, and the Pacific Ocean to the right. The sunset terminator cut the Pacific Ocean in half; everything past Polynesia to his right was in darkness. His view of Australia was cut off by the ribbon, extending down from the car.

He looked up. Perhaps a thousand feet above was the terminus. It was being built by human androids working in the vacuum without the benefit of spacesuits.

Abigail followed his gaze. "We have been bringing pieces of the terminus up even as the ribbon is being built. It is necessary for the mass of the terminus to proceed apace, to hold up the weight of the ribbon."

"And they just walk around out there?"

"We have no need of air, Mr. Vanson. Some of our materials are air-logged, and any internal spaces are filled with air, however, so sudden decompression can be fatal. The ride up is long enough that the necessary decompression and recompression is gradual enough."

"Well, this," he waved his hand out at it all, the stars, the Earth, the terminus and its unsuited and all-too-human workers, "is astounding." He turned to her. "Thank you so much."

"It has been my pleasure, Mr. Vanson. And now if you would, please."

She gestured to the booth, and he got in. Once more, she closed the door. His weight suddenly returned and she reopened the door.

"And we have returned."

"Remarkable."

Having seen all the preparations underway for the evacuation of the flesh-and-blood humans to the colonies, Vanson was eager to see how it all turned out, and he had no need to wait.

Abigail accompanied him back to the church cemetery. His Hummer-esque golf cart was still there, parked on his grandparents' headstone as he had left it.

"So how long, do you think? Fifty years? A hundred? Two hundred?" he asked.

"Fifty or a hundred years would not be long enough. Departure will not be for ten years. It is a fifty-year transit to either of the colonies. We will surreptitiously watch for the first ten years or so, and then it is a fifty-year return trip for us to hear any news. One hundred and fifty years ought to do it. "

"Very well, then. See you in a hundred and fifty years."

Vanson climbed into the time machine, and set the controls. With a last wave, he closed the door, then activated the machine. He reopened the door and climbed out.

He was shocked by what he saw. The cemetery was overgrown, the church in ruins. In fact, most of the town was in ruins. Some of the buildings had been destroyed by a fire. Others had collapsed. The stone courthouse still stood, presiding over the wreckage. Nature was reclaiming the town, starting wherever there was clear earth -- a lawn, a gravel parking lot, a drainage area -- in which to take root.

Abigail sat on the bench, looking no different than when he had left. She looked up as he got out.

"Hello, Mr. Vanson."

"Hi, Abigail." He gestured around at the ruins of the town. "What happened?"

"The project was successful. We evacuated all the humans to the ships. At first, some ten percent or so did not want to leave. Once they understood that ninety percent were going, another half of that ten percent decided to go as well. People kept signing on until the last thousand or two holdouts decided to go with the crowd. By the time it was actually time to depart, everyone was excited to be going. We weren't sure what we would do if there were objections, but ultimately everyone decided to go. We were surprised.

"The trip went without incident. All six ships arrived at their destinations, and the two space elevators deployed properly. Everyone was transported down. Our planning was for the most part correct. They had everything they truly needed in the cargo we sent along. After a few sparse years, the colonies were thriving. Also, humans were reproducing again. That made us very happy." She smiled a sad smile at him.

She went on. "So we withdrew our observers, lest they be spotted."

"That's all good news, but what happened here?"

"This town was no longer needed, Mr. Vanson. It has been abandoned. The current question is yourself. I see basically two options: time and space. You can use the time-stasis field in your vehicle to transport yourself a few hundred years at a time into the future, and see if the human race recolonizes this planet in the future. Or you can travel to the colonies yourself, and resume residence among your own kind. There is a small spaceship available for your use should you desire to take the second option."

"I can't stay here?"

"I think it would be unwise. There are no flesh-and-blood humans on the planet at all. You would be completely cut off from your own kind. I do not think that is a healthy choice."

"Well, let's go look at this spaceship. I can still decide what to do after I look it over, right?"

"Yes, certainly."

He grabbed the backpack with his games out of the time machine and followed her.

They did not go to the airport, but drove the fifty miles to the coast in an SUV. The pavements were cracking and starting to sprout weeds, but the roads were still passable. In drydock lay an ocean-going boat, a 100-foot catamaran with both sloop-rigged sails and twin diesel engines.

Abigail opened the manual drydock valves and the seawater began filling the drydock and lifting the boat.

"There are not sufficient provisions for flesh-and-blood humans on this vessel, so you will need to spend the journey in time-stasis, Mr. Vanson."

"Are you going to be OK piloting this ship to Indonesia by yourself, Abigail?"

"The vessel has a robot pilot and is easy to handle. I don't expect any problems."

Abigail inspected the boat thoroughly while Vanson waited in the captain's chair and brooded. Dark suspicions were forming in his mind, and he pondered hard on his options.

Inspection completed, Abigail returned and started the engines . She engaged the autopilot, and the catamaran began gliding out of the drydock. Once clear, the boat turned to the west, and set off. As Vanson watched, the sails began to deploy, caught the wind, and their speed increased.

"And now, Mr. Vanson, if you would." Abigail gestured to the time-stasis booth, similar to the one he had used on the space elevator, at the back of the cabin.

Vanson climbed into the booth, and said, "Bon voyage."

Abigail closed the door of the booth, and almost immediately opened it again.

"We have arrived."

Vanson got out of the booth and it was much hotter than it had been back in his hometown. He looked out the cabin's forward windscreen and saw that they were tied up at a dock near the gigantic structure of the space elevator. The black ribbon soared off into the sky above.

Vanson looked around as they walked to the space elevator. The once bustling site was now quiet and overgrown. There was no one around at all. There was a car waiting at the bottom of the elevator, a sealed car with an airlock door in the ceiling. Abigail motioned him aboard and into another time-stasis booth. She had gotten quieter and quieter, from the time they had left the cemetery.

Vanson stepped into the booth, and Abigail closed the door. He felt sudden weightlessness, and she opened the door again.

"We have arrived."

She assisted him in cycling the airlock door in the ceiling and moving on into the terminus. They floated through a series of empty corridors within the terminus, to another airlock door, and on into a ship.

Abigail gave him a tour of the ship. It had no sleeping cabins or food dispensers. There was a small sanitation facility, sort of like a space outhouse, clearly for minimal use. The piloting cabin prominently included a half dozen time-stasis booths.

Piloting was simple. There were three buttons, one for Earth, and one for each colony. The ship would automatically detach from the terminus it was currently at, travel to the selected destination, and dock with the elevator terminus there.

The time-stasis booths were similarly simple. There was an activation button that would turn on the time-stasis field until the ship reached its destination. The ship would then release the booth from stasis through control leads to the base on the wall, to which the booth was fastened. The activation button was duplicated, with one both inside and outside each booth.

"So all I do is push the destination button for one colony or the other, and then get into the booth and push the activation button, and when the door opens, I'm there?"

"Yes, that's correct, Mr. Vanson."

Well, it's now or never, Vanson thought. He took her hand in his. "Abigail. Answer a question for me."

"Certainly, Mr. Vanson."

"Where is everybody?"

"As I told you, Mr. Vanson, all the flesh-and-blood humans were shipped off to the colony planets."

"That's not what I asked you, Abigail. Where are all the android humans?"

She avoided his gaze.

He shook her hand. "Abigail?"

She looked back at him. "They -- died."

"Died? How? I would think android humans would have a longer lifespan than flesh-and-blood humans."

"They suicided. Or as good as suicided. They did not recharge themselves."

"In God's name, why?"

"The flesh-and-blood humans created us in their own image, Mr. Vanson. They were more successful than they thought. More successful than *we* thought. The android humans suicided because they had no purpose. The flesh-and-blood humans no longer needed them."

"And you?" Vanson asked.

"There remained one task. To meet you at the appointed time and send you on to the colonies, to be with your own kind. I would not leave you stranded."

"How long did you wait on this planet, alone, after the last other android human died?"

"Twenty-six years," Abigail said.

"Why didn't you use the time-stasis field? You knew when I planned to come back."

"I didn't want to take the chance of missing you."

"And now?" Vanson asked.

Abigail looked away from him and whispered, "My task is done."

The back of Vanson's mind howled with rejection of her implication. "Abigail, come with me."

"I -- I can't. The presence of android humans almost destroyed the human race. The flesh-and-blood humans designed us to perform all their work, relieve them of all drudgery, and they fell into a trap of their own making. How long would it be until that would repeat in microcosm, until you fell into the same trap?"

"Abigail, I'm not asking you to be my servant. I'm asking you to be my wife."

She laid her hand alongside his face. A tear slid down her cheek.

"Mr. Vanson --"

"Craig."

"Craig. I would like to, very much, but I cannot. I can't take the chance that you would, by taking me along, harm yourself. Fall into that same trap."

But isn't that my *decision, dammit?* Vanson thought.

She continued. "And what about the other colonists?"

"Oh, c'mon. We can be that crazy old couple out in the country. No one need know."

"I can't."

"Abigail --"

"No."

She said it with finality.

"All right, all right. You win. I don't even know what I was thinking, trying to argue with you."

She took his face in both hands and, for the first time, kissed him. Not like a friend. Like a lover.

"Don't forget me."

"I won't."

She now had tears running down both cheeks. So did he, for that matter.

"Before you go, can you go over the controls with me one last time?"

"Of course, M-- Craig."

She walked him through the autopilot controls one more time, then showed him the booth controls. As she floated into one of the booths in the zero-gravity to point out the activation button, Vanson closed the door and pushed the external activation button. The booth vanished.

The elevator terminus computer dutifully logged the departure of the ship in docking bay #4. Communications with the ship confirmed the destination as the colony planet Phoenix, with two time-stasis booths occupied.

Adamant

Jane Henderson watched the star field as she adjusted thrust and vector. She was decelerating hard now, aiming for a rendezvous in both time and space with the freight station that would be orbiting Adamant when she got there.

She exulted in the sensation of flying through the star field. Her time sense was skewed both by time dilation at her near-c speed and by the time adjustment she had made to her own perceptions in the piloting computer.

Within the viewer, she was shipless, suitless, bodiless, her mind alone traversing the star field in space, in time, and in gravity, all of which she could see in the five-dimensional display.

She could adjust the five-space viewer to show her the actual view, of the four-mile-diameter ship around her, the blazing artificial singularity miles behind that beckoned the ship into its gravity well, creating the deceleration she required, the stars speed-compressed into an ultraviolet cloud in front of her and an infrared cloud behind. But it was this view that she loved, and it was this view she must use to pilot the ship in the space-time-gravity field.

She was on final approach, decelerating hard, the rendezvous just hours ahead in ship's time, but still days in the future in the sidereal universe.

After one final check of her programming for the approach, Jane slowed her time perception to ship-normal and shut down the viewer. She was once again in the pilot's chair, surrounded by her life-support equipment, enclosed within the armored cocoon behind the bridge. She passed the command to the piloting computer to open the cocoon.

Chon Dawkins turned as the warning sounded, and watched the pilot's cocoon open like a giant clamshell at the back of the bridge. The smell of chemicals and over-oxygenated air hit him as the cocoon cycled fully open.

The Pilot was lying almost prone in the contoured chair in the center, and looked exhausted to the point of death. Ashen, drawn, weak, barely conscious. Of course, that's how the Pilot always looked at the end of a successful crossing, and as captain of the *Jane Henderson*, he had seen it many times. He had been captain for thirty-five ship years, since the ship was commissioned, and always with this Pilot, for the ship was the pilot and the pilot the ship.

The Pilot's attendants disconnected the myriad tubes through which the computer kept the Pilot aspirated, oxygenated, fed, hydrated, and scavenged of carbon dioxide and bodily wastes during the flight, then assisted her out of the chair and into a wheelchair. Jane Henderson was heavier than most human cultures would regard as the optimal human build, as were most pilots. The extra weight helped them survive the physical stresses that piloting put on their bodies. She looked to have lost about twenty pounds on this crossing, which made it about average.

She was completely naked except for her symbiont. Like a large three-legged starfish, the faceless creature sprawled across the top of her hairless head, its three tentacles extending one down her back and one down each arm, reaching all the way onto the backs of her hands. It's color depended somewhat on its mood. It was now a grey-green of exhaustion, like sage in the fall. With her symbiont, the dozen or so physical tube connections -- at her throat, her chest, her forearms, her abdomen, and her groin -- and the metal contacts on her fingertips, you could never mistake her for anything other than a Senior Guild Pilot.

She looked to be about 13 years old. In fact, Dawkins knew, she was just a few years younger in ship time than his own 67 years. In sidereal time, she was much older. Jane Henderson had been born over 400 years ago.

She turned slitted eyes in his direction, and he saluted. She gave him the slightest nod in return. There was nothing to say, he had her report already. She closed her eyes and her attendants wheeled her off the bridge to the pilot's recovery clinic.

Jane Henderson did not wake up in the flotation bed of the pilot's recovery clinic. She woke up on a hard bed in a prison cell. She knew immediately that her symbiont was not with her, as her vision and hearing had the flat ordinariness of an unpaired human.

She did not move, not wanting to give any of her captors who might be watching any indication that she was awake. She could see the hard steel outlines of the cell, in the perennial institutional green that dated from human pre-history. A small metal sink and stool in the corner were the only other furniture she could see in the room other than the bed -- not much more than a cot -- that she was on. She was dressed in an orange shipsuit -- a one-piece unisex coverall -- and nothing else.

She didn't know how the ship had been captured, but it must have been. First, she was aboard a ship of some kind, not on a planet. Human constructs in space always had some slight vibration from the various machinery required to keep man alive in the void. Planetary surfaces had no such vibrations.

So, a ship or station. Her ship had no brig with cells like this. They didn't really have visitors like a station would. Crewmen could be confined to their own quarters through the computer control of all ship's doors. So, not a mutiny. It either had to be a local in-system ship or the freight station she had been setting up rendezvous for. What was the name of the planet again? Without her computer links, without her symbiont, her mind was slow and her memory iffy.

That was another thing. She was without her symbiont. A forced separation could have killed her or the symbiont or both, and she felt no mental or physical trauma, no residue of anything like that. So she had to have been taken while she and her symbiont were voluntarily separated for their recovery. Which meant within a few ship-time days of her going into the recovery clinic.

She was still weak. The recovery process had not completed.

So most likely the station.

Her anger warred with her pity in considering the situation. She was angry, yes, at being taken, being kidnapped, for heaven knew what purpose. But she felt pity, too, for the Guild's response to the kidnapping of a Guild Pilot was likely to be harsh to the point of draconian. The most likely response was to cut the entire colony planet off from interstellar space travel altogether, and let it wither and die over long years of suffering.

She set her pity aside and fed her anger. It would probably be more useful in whatever lay ahead.

Several of the ship's officers were confined in a larger cell nearby.

"What I don't get is what they think they are doing," Jorj Warner, the ship's real-space navigator, said from his perch on the edge of one of the lower bunks. "What can they hope to gain?"

"It looks like an Eternalist rebellion to me, with maybe a bit of 'you're holding us back' thrown in," said Chon Dawkins.

"You're holding us back?" asked Warner.

"There are people who don't understand that you can't turn a colony planet into a Central World overnight. That you have to build up the infrastructure, and it takes time. They resent that the Central Worlds have this or that technology, and they don't. They want it all, and they want it now. Since we are bringing the next stage of infrastructure, and not the whole thing, they feel we are holding them back," said Dawkins.

"But all that Central World technology is massively infrastructure dependent. What are you going to do with a ballistic shuttle, say, without a ballistic shuttleport? And how would you keep it going without enough planetside travel to make it profitable? People gotta eat." Warner said.

"I know, I know, but I think there's some of that here. Mostly, though, I think it's an Eternalist rebellion," said Dawkins.

"You mean those are real?" asked Rikk Monroe, the ship's purser.

"Eternalist rebellions? Sure. Some fellow sells his crop or whatever to a freight station agent, and then ten years later sells again to the same agent, and ten years later, and so on. And the planetside guy is ten years older every time, but the station agent doesn't look a day older. So they're convinced the people on the station have the secret of eternal youth, and won't share it," Dawkins said

"But that's all time dilation! The freight station is only in orbit for several months every ten years. Then it does a long relativistic loop for ten years sidereal, but it's only a few months ship-time. Don't they get that?" Monroe asked.

"Most people, on most planets, do. That's the only way interstellar shipping can work. We haven't been to this planet in over a hundred years sidereal. All of our business contacts from last time are dead.

We age on ship-time, the planetside folks age on sidereal time, and the station residents age on their station's ship-time, which is enough of a happy medium that they can have contacts in both directions and make it work. Most people get that. But fostering hatred and a sense of being taken advantage of by an outside enemy is a great way for a dictator to gain and consolidate power, and it looks like that's what happened here," Dawkins said. "And I don't know any of these people."

"So what?" asked Warner.

"They're not station people, or I think I would recognize somebody from our last time here. I think the station got taken when it came into orbit and made its first contacts with the planet. Its schedule is well known -- it has to be, for them to have cargoes ready -- and I think the station folks probably walked right into it, the same way I did," Dawkins said.

"You couldn't know," said Warner.

"No, but I shouldn't have been such a patsy. The Pilot will not be happy," Dawkins said.

"They took her, too, right?" asked Monroe.

"Yes, they did. But I don't think they took her symbiont. The Pilot and her symbiont would have separated for the initial stages of their recovery, and either these planetside folks didn't find it, or maybe they don't even know about it. And that means they have a big problem," Dawkins said.

"A big problem?" asked Monroe.

"Oh, yes. A very big problem. Because her symbiont is going to come looking for her. And if they get back together, these people are going to find out just how unhappy she is," said Dawkins.

"If she's in a cell like us, what can she do, symbiont or no?" asked Monroe.

"Think about it. This freight station is basically a ship, too, right? It has to be, to do its time dilation loop every ten years. In fact, it was flown here in the first place. So who built this station?" asked Dawkins.

"Well, the Pilots Guild would have built it, right?" asked Warner. His eyes widened. "Oh. Oh! Damn. You know, I almost feel sorry for them. Almost."

Jane Henderson's symbiont woke in its recovery tank, as usual after piloting an interstellar flight. Using its tentacles as both arms and legs, it opened the lid of the tank and moved out onto the table, which was next to the pilot's recovery bed. But, unlike usual -- unlike every other time, in fact -- its partner was not there.

The symbiont expanded its mental senses, scanning the ship. Its partner was not on the ship. Expanded again, out, out --- there! Its partner was not happy. It was angry. And frustrated. And in danger.

The symbiont followed the path back from its partner, and also forward from where it was. Several paths. Some with other beings along them, some, mostly smaller ones, without.

The symbiont eeled off the table to the floor and set out to find its partner.

The brig watch officer delivered food to the prisoners from a wheeled shelving rack. One covered serving dish to each prisoner. Six in this cell, six in this cell, down the row, then, finally, three in this cell, and just one in the last cell. He wheeled the rack back up the corridor to his watch desk, leaving it there for the food service guy to pick up.

In his trip down the brig corridor, he never looked up.

The symbiont was flattened against the ceiling, mimicking the institutional green coloring. This was the hard part, how to get into the room its partner was in. The larger door of the room was solid, no sneaking through. It watched the other being moving down this passageway, and how it slid things into the rooms through the smaller door in the wall. It noted how that door opened.

When the other being was once again bored and inattentive, it slowly worked its way over to the wall, around the corner and down the wall.

Jane Henderson opened one eye as the food slot door slid open once again, and her heart leapt as she saw the tip of a tentacle ease through it. Her symbiont slid through the opening, the primary tentacle first, then the body squeezed through, and finally the secondary tentacles. It sidled over to the bed and slid up into her arms.

It was not a pet. There was no communication, or attempt at communication, between them. They were just too alien, each from the other. But, when joined, they became more than the sum of the parts. Jane had no name for the symbiont, it was a part of her greater self.

She stiffly rose and set the symbiont down on the bed. She peeled off the shipsuit and tossed it aside. She lifted the symbiont by the sides of the body and placed it on her head. The three tentacles sought out their places down her back, down her arms. The symbiont's feeding and discharge tubes engaged the fixtures on either side of her head behind the ears. In its natural habitat, those tubes were inserted into the partner's bloodstream through the skin.

As the symbiont's tentacles took up their positions, she could feel the symbiont's mentality merge with hers. Her vision became sharper, deeper, covered more frequencies, saw more. Her hearing, too, sharpened, picked up more frequencies, became more subtle. Other perceptions came: intuition, spatial awareness, limited scan.

Much of her clarity of mind and memory came back to her. Nothing as it would with connection to the ship, the final assembly of that tripartite being which was Jane Henderson, but for now this would do.

Jane remembered the planet. Adamant. And as she reached out with her perceptions, her "feel" of the structure around her, she recognized it as a Pilots Guild Planetary Freight Station Mark 12 (Colony Edition).

She didn't have the complete plans in her memory, but she did remember some things. She walked around the cell, dragging one tentacled arm along the surface. There! Running horizontally behind the back wall was a wired communications and control line. She aligned her tentacled arm along the surface, felt for the best spot for her fingertips. She tried for an inductive contact along the device bus, and got a query from the station system.

She identified herself to the station as Guild Senior Pilot Jane Henderson, and gave her access code. She had been on Guild rosters when this station was deployed two hundred sidereal years ago, and should be listed in the station's memory. She was recognized and had access, although at the slower speeds of a device link, into the station's computer systems.

She programmed a sensor loop of her cell to repeat the last ten or so minutes before the food had arrived, and used it to wipe the arrival of her symbiont. She also set it up to repeat into the future.

Thus given some protection against detection, Jane began reviewing data. The plans of the station. The location of her ship. Its current status. Total current population on board the station. The whereabouts of each. Who on the station were regular listed personnel, and, more importantly, who were not.

She found where her ship's crew was being held, here in the same brig, and locked their doors against any entry without her permission. That should make them safe from their captors for now. She also flickered the light in her captain's cell twice, then, five seconds later, once more.

"That is very interesting," Chon Dawkins said, looking up as the lights flickered twice. Jorj Warren and Rikk Monroe raised their eyebrows, but Dawkins just winked at them and held up a silencing finger. When the lights flickered once more, Dawkins smiled. "And I think life is about to get very interesting for our hosts."

Jane Henderson stepped over to the door and felt for the location of the door controls on the other side of the wall. Once she found them, she located her fingertips on the wall very precisely. She took up position immediately inside the door, and then manipulated the controls.

Bron Pavich liked brig duty. Not much to do, all of it seated. None of this standing guard, or patrolling here, there, and everywhere. Nice, quiet, no action. But he still got to wear the black shipsuit that was the space-deployed uniform of the GP -- the General Police, the planetary government's enforcement arm -- and enjoy the perks that went with it. No one got in his way, no one asked what he was doing. Ordinary citizens wanted as little involvement with the GP as possible.

BAM!

That shouldn't happen. All the cell doors were closed and locked, so how could a cell door slam? And the cell doors were motorized, like most station doors, and had a fixed rate of closure except in cases of pressure leak. How could it slam?

He drew his sidearm and walked slowly down the empty hall, pellet pistol in hand.

BAM!

It was the door at the end of the hall, the solitary confinement cell. Bron walked up to the door, and as he watched, the door slid open about three inches and slammed again.

BAM!

What a weird failure! He looked at the controls, then pushed the "Close" icon.

When the "Close" icon was pushed, the door instead shot open at maximum speed. Jane grabbed the guard's gun wrist in one hand while the tentacle from her other arm slashed out and wrapped itself around the guard's head across the eyes. She felt for the volition centers of his mind, and killed them. Bron Pavich stopped struggling. She released him, and he stood docilely.

Where to? The station was originally flown here. There would have been a pilot's chair for that trip, but it would have been removed when the station was placed in orbit. The simple loop it flew every ten years sidereal would run on autopilot. She would be protected once inside her own ship, assuming she could get there. She knew through her symbiont's earlier scans that there were guards at the dock entry. She also knew she would never be close to fitting through the unguarded air ducts and serviceways her symbiont had used.

So the dock entry would have to be it.

Jane Henderson walked down the brig corridor, naked except for her symbiont, and the automaton that had been Bron Pavich followed, sidearm still held down at his side.

Chon Dawkins, Rikk Monroe, and Jorj Warner heard the neighboring cell door slam several times, then quiet.

"And so it starts," Dawkins said.

"OK, so she's a pilot, I get that. But what can she really do? Even if she can control the ship and the station, she can only do that if she gets to a terminal, right? And what about the guards?" asked Monroe.

"Pilots get a lot of training, in a lot of different areas. Since they can live inside the computer, in computer time, they have a lot of time for training and simulations while the surgical modifications are done for their life-support hookups. And don't forget that that symbiont of hers has a lot of mental abilities we don't understand. I don't know near all of it -- Guild pilots just don't talk about it -- but I know enough. Every once in a while, a pilot will fall into psychosis, and the results are not pretty. I had to help clean up from one of those when I was in officer training, and it was horrific," Dawkins said. He stared off into the distance as some memory came back to him, then shook it off.

"And Guild pilots have a sort of strange attitude toward life. Jane Henderson was born some 400 sidereal years ago. All of the people she knew as a child are dead. Her parents, siblings, aunts, uncles -- every planetside person she knew is dead. Same for us, I suppose. But Guild pilots are more isolated. The next time she comes through this system, in fifty or a hundred or a hundred and fifty years, all of these people will be dead. If they die now or die later, it makes little difference to her.

"No, they thought she was helpless in that cell. But she had to have hooked back up with her symbiont and penetrated the station systems to flicker the cell lights here and give me that signal. And joined with her symbiont, she's not helpless. Angry, maybe, but not helpless. I'm just as glad we're in here, frankly. This could get really messy."

They reached the docking entry without incident, Jane Henderson walking ahead and the automaton following, sidearm drawn and hanging at his side. Some people gawked at her nakedness, her symbiont, her life-support connections, but she didn't give a damn. No one made any effort to interfere with what was obviously a helpless prisoner being transferred by an armed guard in a black GP shipsuit. She had kept scanning ahead -- firearms were easy to spot in a mental scan -- and only once had they had to duck into a doorway on a side corridor until a GP patrol had passed.

As they approached the docking entry, she saw the two guards, one on either side of the access hatch, both with the same black GP shipsuits and sidearms as her escort. The guards watched them cross the open area to the hatch. Just as they were about to challenge her escort, she dropped to the deck and the automaton lifted his pistol and hosed the guards with a stream of mag-driven explosive pellets. The effect at a distance of less than fifteen feet was horrendous.

Now spattered with blood and bits, Jane picked herself up off the deck and walked forward to the hatch controls. She opened the hatch and walked through into her ship's docking tube without looking back. As she passed into her ship, she released her control of the automaton, and he who had been Bron Pavich fell dead to the deck.

Jane Henderson crawled back into the pilot's chair of her ship and plugged into the life-support systems. As she closed the armored cocoon, she considered what to do next. The umbilicals of the ship had not been connected to the station, but that was no matter. She connected to the station's computer systems through the data connections made automatically by the attachment of the docking tube. Now tied into the ship's computer, she slowed her own time sense down by a factor of several hundred, effectively stopping the world around her.

First, she accessed the security systems and selected video loops for both the docking entry and the brig watch desk, wrote them over her escape, and queued them forward. That should keep anyone from seeing what had happened by looking at the security video. She dispatched station housecleaning robots to the docking entry to clean up and recycle the bodies.

Next, she sent out a recall message to the automated factory container she had dropped off on her way in-system. She had been in recovery already when it separated, but she had set up the drop as part of her approach maneuvers. The four-mile diameter cylinder six miles long was the cargo, or rather the cargo container, she had brought to the system. It had been dropped when it would be able to use its small engines to match velocities with a large asteroid in the outer system -- only the powerful but much smaller interstellar tow boat that was the real *Jane Henderson* had continued on to the station. The factory was actually a meta-factory -- a factory that produces factories -- and was the next step in building up the infrastructure of the colony, using the asteroid for raw materials. But she might need that manufacturing capability. She set up a route that would allow it to pick up several smaller asteroids on the way, and sent the recall message.

Then, she dispatched several repair robots on the station, getting them in position for the upcoming confrontation. She also programmed them to do some minor modifications here and there on the station.

Finally, she dispatched a stealthed Guild communications node, a Pilots Guild Comm Pack Mark 53 (Stealth), to the planet.

With things in motion and no immediate action to be taken, she set out to fill the information gap she had been operating in. She reviewed security videos of the capture of the ship. The crew had been entirely too trusting. She might have to speak to Captain Dawkins about that, but she suspected he was already beating himself up over it. She then reviewed the capture of the station itself. Once again, too trusting, too dependent on routine without enough caution. Finally, she reviewed what was available on the station about the planet's political situation, going back through ten years of news feeds, and found it depressingly familiar.

A charismatic populist politician had risen to power by fanning the flames of resentment against an outside enemy, this time the Pilots Guild. They had all the technology, and were holding it back from The People. In particular, that technology included immortality, life itself, which was a right of all The People. Look at how the station folks hardly aged at all. Yes, he had pictures to prove it. And the spacers aged even less. He had ridden this wave of resentment all the way to high planetary office, and then consolidated power ruthlessly.

He hadn't done it alone. There were always people susceptible to this sort of demagoguery. There were also those who were drawn to power like moths to flame, and enabled this sort of disease to spread. What had been a blooming democracy on the planet had turned into the worst sort of totalitarianism. Yet again, black uniformed secret police terrified a civilian population that had voted its rights away.

The hell of it was, the "Glorious Leader" was at least partially right. The Guild did hold technology that it was not ready to share, yet, with Adamant. It wouldn't do them any good. Truly useful technology was built on layers and layers of infrastructure over time. A portable communicator was useless without a communications net, as a simple example.

The apparent long lifetimes of station and ship crews were due to relativistic time dilation. In ship-time, they lived about as long as anybody else. They weren't quite as exposed to communicable diseases, so they fared a little better, but not much.

The Guild did have some secrets about living a very long time, though, and Jane Henderson was living proof of it. She wondered how many of those planetside folks would want to go through what she had gone through to achieve it. Complete sterility, for one. All those reproductive bits, male and female, required a lot of the body's metabolic energy. They were prone to disease as well. And the sex hormones drove a lot of the aging process. So all pilots were surgically sterilized well before the onset of puberty.

There was much, much more. The nanobots that kept her arteries clear, nipped cancer in the bud, and repaired aneurysms and circulatory weak spots. The abandonment of traditional human foods for formulated nutrition, inserted through surgically implanted connections. The re-engineering of the genes that controlled aging. The fixing of her apparent age at early puberty.

All of it was hideously expensive, but not as expensive as the pilots themselves. Only one in a billion or so people had both the quirk that allowed them to pair with the symbionts that humans had discovered on Bascomb's World *and* the mental ability to use the five-space viewer, *both* of which were required to be a pilot. That was why every human child -- every human child, everywhere -- was tested at age four for the potentials that indicated these abilities were present or could be developed. The Guild paid huge prizes for these children, children just such as Jane Henderson had been four hundred years ago. If a ship came back from a run such as this one to Adamant with a single such child, the crew could retire in splendor, and the colony would get a serious injection to its planetary accounts. The parents could go overnight from obscure poverty to being the wealthiest people on the colony.

In monetary terms alone, Jane Henderson was worth more to the Guild than the ship, the automated factory container, and the station itself, combined, many times over. All of these could be built by robot factories working asteroids, but a potential Guild Pilot was the proverbial needle in a haystack. And without pilots, space travel was long, slow, expensive, and dangerous. Even over well-plotted interstellar courses, robot ships had a percentage survival rate per hop in the single digits. Normal humans fared worse than that.

So keeping a pilot alive as long as possible justified huge expense, and drastic procedures. Is that what those planetside people wanted for themselves?

That was their problem. Jane Henderson's problem was what to do about the entire situation. Regaining her crew and getting them all away unharmed was paramount. What to do about the planet was another matter. She could put a Guild embargo on the system and let them live or die on their own, she supposed, but she knew she couldn't leave it at that. It would be too cruel to the majority of the population that just wanted to get on with their lives. She saw no alternative. She would have to take over the planet.

First things first, however.

Brigadier General Brin Denton lounged in the station master's chair in the station control center. It had been *Major* Denton's plan that had captured the station when it returned to orbit after its last ten-year absence. His success had resulted in his recent promotion to the general staff. He straightened his uniform jacket. GP enlisted men and officers wore black shipsuits when deployed in space, but general staff always wore their normal uniforms. He had had the foresight to obtain and bring along a brigadier general's uniform when he moved to take the station. One can't be too careful about appearances, after all.

And now he had captured a Guild ship undamaged *and* the Guild Pilot unharmed!

The station command center was set up like the bridge of a starship. The station master's command chair, on a slight dais, faced the large main display. The main display was pretty much the entire wall in front of him, and took the place of the large forward windows on the bridge of a sea-faring ship planetside. The various department consoles and their staff were arrayed in an arc between him and the display. An open area behind him had once held a temporary Guild pilot's chair, but that had been removed once the station was delivered.

The main display was currently showing an outside view of the Guild starship docked with his station. *His* starship, he mentally corrected himself, and smiled.

"Sir, we're being hailed," communications officer Jasn Devon said.

"By whom?" Denton asked.

"By the *Jane Henderson*, Sir."

"But there's nobody on that ship."

"She says she's Guild Senior Pilot Jane Henderson."

"Pull up the security view of her cell!"

In the security view now displayed on the viewscreen, Jane Henderson slept on the cell bed in the orange prison shipsuit.

"Get someone down to the brig. Make sure she is actually there."

"She's still hailing, Sir."

"Put her on the screen."

The viewscreen now showed a mature woman of indeterminate age, standing on a headland overlooking an ocean, wearing a long, white, belted dress. Her salt-and-pepper waist-length hair was blowing slightly in an on-shore breeze, her long-sleeved arms hanging simply at her sides. She wore a worldly-wise and patient expression, like your mother when you'd misbehaved. Denton did not recognize the image as that of a Celtic witch, but it was unsettling nonetheless.

"That's not you, that's a stupid avatar," Denton said.

"A simple affectation, General Denton. Of course, it's an avatar, as I have no intention of showing you the interior of my ship," Jane Henderson's avatar said.

"*My* ship, you mean. But you hailed me, so to what do I owe the pleasure?"

"I called to discuss surrender terms, General."

"I'll tell you my terms. Unconditional surrender. You will exit your ship and place yourself back in my custody immediately."

"I called to discuss the terms of *your* surrender, General."

"*My* surrender? You must be crazy, lady. You are one person, in a ship that is docked to my station, and under my guns. I hold your crew. I have plenty of ships and men to deal with one jumped-up Guild pilot."

"You will not surrender to me?" the avatar asked.

"Not in a million years. What I will do is start killing your crew, one at a time, live on this comm channel, if you do not surrender to me within five minutes."

"That is the wrong answer." The avatar closed its eyes and lifted its head, spread its hands out at its sides.

One second, General Denton was sitting back in his command chair looking at the viewscreen. The next, he was spasming violently in the chair, hair sticking out from his head, electrical sparks shooting from his hair, his hands, his feet. Electrical discharges raced up and down his uniform. Then he was still, his body smoking, while the smell of ozone and voided sphincters drifted across the room.

"I would like to convey my respects to your new station commander on his very recent promotion, Mr. Devon," the avatar said, looking directly at the communications officer.

Jasn Devon gulped several times before he could speak. The avatar waited patiently. "Y-yes, Ma'am. I'll have to call him, Ma'am, h-he's off duty right now."

"Please do, Mr. Devon."

Colonel Nikk Sheffield, also newly promoted, was shocked to hear of Denton's death. He wasn't sure how the Guild pilot had killed Denton, but he wasn't going to let it happen to him. The best defense was a good offense. So he ordered his men into battle gear, and sent a couple of squads to bring the senior prisoners up to the command center.

They found that the cell doors would not open for them, so he sent a crew with a plasma cutter down to the brig to cut the cell doors open.

Jane Henderson was monitoring all of the security cameras inside the station. It looked like Colonel Sheffield was going to be no smarter than General Denton had been. He was doing her the favor of concentrating his forces in the barracks, where they were donning battle gear, and in the brig, where they were setting up a plasma cutter.

She waited for the opportune moment. Meanwhile, she hailed the station again.

"She's hailing us, Sir," communications officer Jasn Devon said.

The remains of General Denton had been removed from the still smoking command chair. Colonel Sheffield stood in front of the chair and faced the viewscreen.

"Put her on the screen," Sheffield said.

The avatar appeared on the screen again, and Jasn Devon noted that there was a storm developing over the ocean behind her. It didn't look like a good sign to him.

"Colonel Sheffield, I am prepared to accept your surrender," the avatar said.

"Well, you're not going to get it. My men are rigging for battle right now, and your crew is being brought up here where I will shoot them one at a time right in front of you if *you* don't surrender to *me*," Sheffield said.

"I see you're a slow learner. Very well. On your head be it."

Fire on a space station is as dangerous as fire on a seagoing ship. All the more curious, since a seagoing ship was surrounded by water, and a space-faring vessel was surrounded by vacuum, both inimical to fire. Pumping ocean water onto a ship to fight a fire was common. In a similar vein, vacuum could be used to fight fire on a space station.

But vacuum was a lot faster.

A couple of hours after Chon Dawkins figured that Jane Henderson had made her escape, the intercom speakers in the brig cells came to life.

"Crew, this is Jane. The station people are failing to show the proper respect due a Senior Guild Pilot, but I hope to have that rectified shortly. In the meantime, do not try to open your cell doors, and make sure your food slot doors are properly closed. There will for a time be a lack of air in the corridor."

The station command center viewscreen image shifted suddenly from Jane Henderson's avatar to the brig watch station and the corridor beyond. Colonel Sheffield saw his men standing in the watch station while a small crew was setting up a plasma cutter in the hallway. He could hear them talking as they waited.

Then there was the sudden slam of airtight doors, followed by the howling of air as a fire control valve opened, discharging the air in the compartment to space. The howl faded as the air necessary to carry the sound bled away.

Sheffield gaped at the horrific scene as his troops were effectively spaced in place.

The viewscreen image shifted again, to one of the GP barracks on the station. His black-shipsuited GP troops were donning body armor and being issued weapons.

"No. No," Sheffield whispered, as the scene inexorably unfolded again, and again, and again, airtight doors closing, fire control valves opening, and his troops dying, in all three GP barracks on the station, one at a time, before his eyes.

The screen shifted back to the avatar standing on the headland.

"Your surrender, Colonel Sheffield?" the avatar asked.

"No! Never! I'll never surrender! I'll come down there and kill you myself! You can't do this! You're one person! You're nothing! I'll kill you! I'll kill you!" Colonel Sheffield ranted, foam drooling from the corners of his mouth, and his eyes mad.

"Two can play with plasma cutters, Colonel Sheffield," the avatar said softly.

A single pulse of a plasma cutter beam burst through the ceiling above Colonel Sheffield's head and passed straight down through his body. The superheated core of his body turning to plasma literally blew him apart, showering the command center and its occupants with bits of the former GP colonel.

"Won't anybody surrender to me?" the avatar said with a sigh.

Jasn Devon held up a hand at his comm terminal, much as a schoolboy with the right answer. "I will, Ma'am. I'd be happy to surrender."

Stationmaster Jaym Berwick and a couple dozen of his crew had gathered in the recreation area of the residential wing where they had been imprisoned by the GP since the station had been captured. They had felt the slight jar of the station when each of the fire control valves had been opened. That was something that, once felt, was never forgotten. Then, about fifteen minutes later, a series of subtle drops in station pressure as evacuated areas were re-pressurized. Something big was up, but what? Was the station on fire?

The intercom came to life. "Stationmaster Berwick, this is Senior Guild Pilot Jane Henderson. I have retaken control of this space station. General Denton and Colonel Sheffield are dead. The station command center has surrendered to me and is locked down. Most GP forces on the station are dead. It seems they didn't know anything about fire control procedures aboard a space station."

Berwick's crew, stunned to silence by events, laughed at that last, then cheered.

"I now return command of this space station to you, Stationmaster. There are some remaining GP forces on the station, but I can get you safely to the GP barracks where you can obtain body armor and weapons. Until all GP troops are accounted for, I recommend caution." Jane paused, and the door from the recreation center to the rest of the station opened. In the doorway, a construction robot with a heavy plasma cutter hovered on anti-grav. Two GP troopers who had been guarding the door lay dead in the corridor beyond, nearly blown in half. "This robot will escort you to the nearest GP barracks where you can pick up body armor and weapons. I'm afraid you may have to clean them off a bit.

"And remember, spacers. The people in the command center have surrendered to my authority and are under my protection. They are to be escorted to the brig, where they can occupy the cells my crew are currently in. I would also appreciate my crew being escorted back to my ship with protection against any remaining GP who might be roaming around."

On the way to the GP barracks, the station crew had twice run into GP patrols. The robot had twice demonstrated the ineffectiveness of body armor against the pulse mode of a heavy plasma cutter.

As the robot approached the GP barracks, the double doors slid aside, revealing a scene straight out of hell. About a hundred and fifty GP troops lay on the floor in the contortions of death by sudden vacuum. Most of the bodies were not intact, having burst from internal pressure. Blood and burst organs were everywhere. The smell was indescribable.

Berwick turned back to his crew. "OK, anybody who can stomach this for a few seconds, we need those weapons, and I think there are some armored vests on the tables there. We could use those as well. I'm asking for volunteers. No censure of anyone who can't." With that, he turned and walked into the room.

A dozen or so crew followed him, but two had to turn back, retching. The others did manage to get enough weapons and armored vests to outfit them all, then the doors mercifully closed on the abattoir of General Police Barracks Number 2.

As Berwick was donning his vest, he called to the ceiling. "Senior Guild Pilot, are you there?"

"Yes, Stationmaster. I am monitoring."

"Could you dispatch housekeeping robots to the GP barracks to clean up the bodies?"

"Certainly, Stationmaster. Specifics, please."

"Recycle the bodies. Clean and retain the remaining weapons and armored vests. Clean and retain undamaged uniforms. Clean and disinfect the room."

"The uniforms, Stationmaster?"

"We may need some, I think, if we have to impersonate GP personnel for communications or even visitors. Just seems prudent to hang onto some of them."

"Understood and agreed. I'll send some housekeeping robots to the brig as well. Henderson out."

Berwick turned back to his crew. "All right. Jacobs, take a half dozen crew down to the brig and release the Guild ship crew, but keep them there until we can clear a path to their ship. Get them any food or anything they need. Make sure they're hydrated. Survey them and advise me of any injuries or medical needs.

"Smitty, take a half dozen crew down to the brig, then make a trial run to the ship and back and clear any GP you run into. Don't take any chances. Let this robot take point. Just call out directions at corridor intersections so the Senior Guild Pilot can steer the robot ahead of you. Once you've completed that, call me and give me a threat assessment for taking the Guild crew back to their ship.

"Bannon, take a half dozen of the tech types with you and get down to main engineering. Survey our situation there and see what those GP monkeys have left us with. Start with environmental. Let's make sure we aren't in trouble for air.

"I'll take a group of watch standing crew with me to the command center and we will run diagnostics on the whole station and get things back in order there. All right. Sort yourselves out and get about it."

Jane Henderson readjusted her time sense so she was running only about four times faster than real time. This still allowed her to monitor her ship's crew, as well as the station crew teams as they performed Berwick's assignments. Other security cameras were now being monitored by software.

It was only about three hours sidereal since she had been incarcerated, but that had been days in her personal time, and she had not completed recovery from the inbound flight. She knew she had taken the direct route to her goals, and that, had she been rested, she may have been able to achieve those goals with less loss of life. But perhaps not. The GP was a volunteer outfit: every one of the dead had signed up to wear the black uniform of the oppressor. And none of the good guys had been killed. So she hadn't been *that* sloppy. Still, eight survivors -- the station command center crew -- out of almost 500 GP personnel on board the station did seem kind of overkill.

But she had had to hurry. Even with her life support racing to keep up with removing fatigue products from her system, she was in a race against her own diminishing ability to function. And when you got right down to it, they were the ones that took her prisoner, not the other way around.

"C'mon guys, let's get this done," she muttered. "I'm about done in."

As Chon Dawkins, once more captain of the *Jane Henderson*, and his crew took up their bridge positions, the warning bell sounded. Dawkins stood and turned as the clamshell of the pilot's chair opened. *God, she looks like hell*, Dawkins thought as her attendants unplugged her life support fittings and assisted her to her wheelchair. She and her symbiont were both ashen. Once seated, Jane Henderson half-opened her eyes to look at him. Rather than saluting as before, Dawkins slightly bowed his head and spread his hands out at his sides. *I'm sorry I screwed up.* Jane Henderson lifted just the fingers of her right hand in a little wave of dismissal. *Apology accepted.*

Her attendants turned her around and headed her off to the recovery clinic.

It was almost a week before Jane Henderson left the recovery clinic. She had sent notice to Dawkins for an update briefing as soon as she came out, and he had arrived in the briefing room early.

It had been a busy week. Stationmaster Berwick had the station mostly back up to his own persnickety standards. Space habitats had their own ways of weeding out the incautious, and Berwick wasn't one of them. The crews of General Denton's in-system ships docked at the station had surrendered when Berwick pointed out that the Guild had built their ships as well, and they were no more immune to vacuum than their comrades had been. Transmitting the video of Jane's brutal attack on the GP barracks had closed the deal.

At Dawkins' request, Berwick had also kept up normal official communications with the planet. The GP communications officer had been a big help in keeping the transition seamless. He wasn't one of the true believer GP types, he just liked the equipment and his father had wangled him the appointment. There was a lockdown on the private communications channels, though, so no news of what had happened here had leaked to the planet. Yet.

Dawkins also had the *Jane Henderson* back up to his own careful standards. He had been luckier than Berwick, as the GP had left the ship alone. There were fewer things for him to set in order than the stationmaster had had to deal with. The ship had been refueled and restocked from station stores and awaited only her mistress's orders.

For, even though Dawkins was the captain, the *Jane Henderson* was under the direct orders of Senior Guild Pilot Jane Henderson. Guild pilots were too aloof, too often incapacitated in recovery, too often operating at different time rates, to actually captain a ship. The crew needed someone in authority, the senior among them. A Guild pilot was never "among them", they were apart from and different than the crew. Henderson thought of the Guild pilots, and Senior Guild Pilot Jane Henderson in particular, like an admiral on a flagship. Apart from the crew, and in authority over the ship.

Jane Henderson had picked Dawkins for her captain, though he was young for the job at the time, on the basis of personal chemistry alone. She had also chosen his first exec. Donl Iverson had been much older and more experienced, and had mentored Dawkins in mastering the role of captain. Jane had thought her relationship with her captain more important than experience, and she had been proven right, at least in this case.

Lizz Ferrano, his current exec, came into the briefing room and took a seat. Tough, capable, and thirty years his junior, she would eventually captain her own ship. Unlike Dawkins, she was tall and lithe: her ballet dancer's body contrasted with Dawkins' heavy frame. Where he was blond-haired and coffee-colored, she was dark-haired and olive-complected. She and the other women officers and crew had been segregated in the brig cells on the station, which showed just how "planetside" their captors had been. It was as ridiculous as segregating people by skin color, or by eye color. To spacers, who lived their entire lives in the most unforgiving environment known to man, the only thing that mattered was competence.

"G'morning, Lizz."

"Good morning, Sir."

"Did Mayr release Thompson from sick bay yet?"

"Yes, Sir, she signed him out a couple hours ago. He was the last. Ship's crew now all fit for duty, ship's stores all topped off."

"Excellent."

He was about to say more when the briefing room door slid open again and Jane Henderson walked in. She was dressed, like them, in the pale green shipsuit used for normal duty on the *Jane Henderson*. Her pallor gone, she was back to her normal tawny complexion, and she looked to have gained back some of the weight she had lost on the flight in to Adamant. Her symbiont, too, had recovered its normal complexion, the grass green of contentment.

Dawkins and Ferrano both stood, and she waved them to be seated as she took the seat at the head of the table.

"First, I want to compliment you both on getting the crew and the ship back in shape so quickly. That was good work."

She would have consulted their reports on the terminal in her recovery clinic. Jane Henderson never showed up unprepared. This briefing was for them, not for her.

"Thank you, Ma'am," Dawkins said, and Ferrano nodded.

"Shifting topics, have either of you looked into what has been happening on the planet the last five or six years?"

"Eternalist rebellion, isn't it, Ma'am?" Dawkins asked.

"Yes and no. They elected a populist government that was pushing all that drivel, but from there this Marc Shluter has taken them to totalitarianism -- government control of everything, secret police, monitoring and surveillance, jailing or killing political and media opposition. Complete police state, one-man control." Jane looked from Dawkins to Ferrano and back. "And we're not going to leave it like that.

"So here's what I want to do."

The larger briefing was a couple of hours later. Stationmaster Jaym Berwick was present, as well as his exec, Katy Bannon. Unlike Dawkins and Ferrano, they were both of medium height and build, but where Bannon was very pale, almost white, with dark, dark eyes, Berwick was as black as space with startling glacier blue-white eyes.

Pleasantries were exchanged and they were all getting seated when Jane Henderson walked in. It was rare for Jane to ever meet with off-ship visitors, but this was different. Berwick and Bannon were both Guild employees. In some sense, Berwick's space station was another ship in Jane's little fleet. Being Guild employees, they weren't at all startled by the Guild Senior Pilot's appearance, her apparent age, or her short, heavy stature.

They all popped back to their feet.

"Be seated, please. Stationmaster Berwick, XO Bannon, welcome to my ship."

"Glad to be aboard, Ma'am," Berwick said.

"Yes, Ma'am. Thank you, Ma'am," Bannon said.

"OK, so, right to business. The issue at hand is what do we do next," Jane said. "The Guild can pull out, and leave Adamant and its people to fend for themselves. This ship has more than enough tow capacity to take the factory container and the station with us when we leave. They are both Guild property under lease to Adamant under a contract that the Adamant government has broken. We can either space the GP prisoners or release them with an in-system ship to take them planetside. I don't care either way.

"Maybe in a hundred years the Guild can come back and see how they're doing, and decide then whether we can start over with whatever's left or not.

"The other option, as I see it, is to take over the planet. That means take down the government, kill this Shluter asshole, kill a whole bunch of GP, empty the concentration camps, drop weapons to the citizens -- basically, kick over the whole anthill and see what comes out of that. We can give the people of Adamant a chance to clean up their own mess, but I am not going to risk Guild personnel to do it. And that means it won't be without collateral damage.

"I don't see any intermediate options. We either go in, or we pull out, but either way, we do it all the way. Opinions?"

Jane looked to the station personnel. Berwick was thoughtful. Bannon had a question.

"Can you really do that? Take out the government, I mean?"

Berwick answered for Jane. "With a Guild factory ship? Oh, she can do it, all right. That is, assuming you have the full software loadout for the factory ship, Ma'am."

"Yes, we have the full loadout. We can make as much of anything as we want, to current Central World tech levels."

"*Current* Central World tech levels? As of your departure?" Bannon asked.

"Current as of twenty-five years or so ago, yes," Jane answered.

"Oh. OK. Yeah, it should be no problem then. That's probably a hundred-year tech advantage over anything the planet can muster," Bannon said.

"Probably pulling out is the wise course, Ma'am, but I don't like it," Berwick said. "I deployed here with this station. We've done maybe twenty port calls in that time, what with our ten-year time-dilation loops. And for the most part, I've liked the planetsiders I've met. I've seen them grow old, met their kids, grandkids, great-grandkids, and dealt with each generation in turn. They're good people, by and large. They just got sucked in by this Shluter character. Every once in a while, one of these sociopathic geniuses comes along, and people can fall for it.

"So I think, all in all, I would prefer to do something if we can."

"XO?" Jane asked.

Bannon was lost in thought. "Huh? Oh, yes, Ma'am. I think I agree with Stationmaster Berwick. Yes, they voted this guy in, but he's been using Guild technology to terrorize his own people. I guess it would just leave a bad taste in my mouth to go ahead and pull out without even trying to do something about it."

"So we're all agreed then, that we see if we can't fix this mess?"

"Well, you're the senior Guild representative in the system, Ma'am, so it's your decision, but I appreciate being consulted. And yes, we agree," Berwick said.

"We've broken into the Guild ship's computer systems, and we've determined that the Guild ship has the software aboard for this space factory to build current Central World technology. There's some great stuff in there, just about anything we could want. We've called the factory ship to come and rendezvous with us, but, with its small engines, it'll take weeks to get here. I could just send the Guild ship out to meet it under Colonel Sheffield, but all in all I think it's better to take the station along. This allows me to be on-site to oversee the initial production, and it also means we have the manpower and warehouse space to take best advantage. The Guild ship is just too small to take significant people along, and it has very limited hold space.

"On other matters, we have not yet completed repairs on the antenna array that was damaged in taking the Guild ship, so we have reserved the limited bandwidth available to official communications for now. We are going to have to maintain a lockdown on private communications with the station for the time being.

"Brigadier General Brin Denton, out."

"Do you think they'll buy the Pilot's avatar of General Denton?" Ferrano asked.

Dawkins looked at his exec, sitting at her console next to his captain's chair. "Sure, why not? It's nothing more than what they want to hear. And all we really need to do is slow them down until we can get the station out of range of them." He consulted his local screen. "Are we ready for departure?"

"Yes, Sir. All departments reporting ready."

Jane Henderson was plugged into her pilot's chair, the cocoon closed. She opened up the five-space viewer, and her cocoon, her life-support equipment, her pilot's chair, and even her body itself left her awareness. All she was aware of was what the five-space viewer showed her, the glorious perception of being physically in space, the station behind her, the planet on her right. She saw the sun, the planets, the moons of the system, where they were, where they would be. The familiar wave of elation came over her.

She also saw the factory ship, 250 million miles distant and slowly thrusting in her direction.

When Dawkins' "Good to go" message came to her, she started building the singularity, spinning it up until it was a blazing diamond in front of her. Slowly she moved away from the planet. As she gained distance from the planet's gravity well, she fed more power into the singularity, increased the pace of her acceleration.

Flying once more.

"Boy, she's in a hurry!" Ferrano said as she consulted her display.

"I think she really wants to get the station out of their range before they wake up to what's really going on," Dawkins said. He smiled. "And I also think she's really enjoying herself, having an excuse to pour it on like this."

"Hey, what's a couple thousand gravities among friends?" Ferrano said, rolling her eyes, and Dawkins chuckled.

Just short of halfway to the factory container, it was time for turnover. This did not involve flipping the ship over, as there was no way the ship could swing that singularity around. Instead, Jane orbited the ship and station a half-turn around the singularity to begin her deceleration.

"Well, I have to say, this is pretty exhilarating. It's been a long time," Stationmaster Berwick told his exec.

"I'd forgotten how quick a Guild tow running light can be," Bannon said.

"And I'm happy for it. I haven't enjoyed the last week being in missile range of those bastards."

"Can't argue with you there, Sir."

Jane was pulling energy back out of the singularity now, slowing the deceleration to match velocities with the still-thrusting factory container. She was backing onto one of the container's forward-facing docking ports, to which she would dock the station. She had to time her deceleration to go past zero velocity with respect to the planet far behind, and re-accelerate up to the relative velocity of the station as it continued in-system. She then let its small acceleration bring it up behind them.

Ferrano watched the container continue to grow in the viewscreen.

"I thought the station was big compared to the *Jane Henderson*, but that thing is enormous. It's like docking with a planet," Ferrano said.

"Not quite, but I know what you mean," Berwick said.

Even though the front circular face of the container filled the entire viewscreen, features on its surface were still growing larger. In the center of the screen he could see docking port #2. Actually, what he saw was an enormous "2", in the center of which was a cluster of small blemishes, the docking port and its clamps and umbilicals.

It kept growing until the docking port passed off the bottom of the viewscreen. After several minutes, there was a small shudder that ran through the station.

"Our docking port #4 reports docking successful. We're locked on," Ferrano said.

"Excellent. Communications, report docking successful to the *Jane Henderson*, and thank them for the ride," Berwick said.

"Yes, Sir," said Jasn Devon, now wearing a station-standard light-blue shipsuit.

"The station reports docking successful, Captain, and thanks us for the ride," Ferrano said.

"Good, good. Thank you, Exec," Dawkins said.

The warning bell sounded and Dawkins stood and walked around his chair as the Pilot's clamshell opened. Jane Henderson's attendants unplugged her life-support tubes and assisted her out of the chair, but she waved off the wheelchair.

"That's OK, Matt, Frannie, I'm fine. Short hop like that, I'm not even winded," Jane said.

Standing naked next to her pilot's chair, she looked over to Dawkins, and nodded.

"You've always had a light touch when docking with containers, Ma'am, but I don't think I've ever seen you do it with one underway before," Dawkins said.

"It's not really all that different, Captain. Everything is always moving with respect to everything else in space anyway." Jane shrugged. "If you need me, I'll be in my quarters."

The *Jane Henderson* spent the next three weeks docked to the station, which was in turn docked to the factory container. Two weeks into that, the container flipped over to bring its thrusters around to the front and begin decelerating. It was still almost five weeks to the planet, which was heading away from them in its orbit.

Jane Henderson spent most of the first two weeks in her quarters, connected into the ship's computer systems. She couldn't use the five-space viewer or control the ship's engines from there, but that wasn't what she needed at the moment. Instead she began a crash-course in military strategy and tactics, together with a review of the use of the weapons systems she would be adding to the *Jane Henderson.*

The Guild had included a number of courses in the ship's library against this sort of situation. Basic Strategy, Intermediate Strategy, Basic Tactics, Intermediate Tactics, the Psychology of Warfare, Logistics, Asymmetric Warfare and more.

Some days she went to the bridge and took to her pilot's chair to practice simulations. The Guild had included five-space viewer recordings or reconstructions from past engagements. Here she practiced ship maneuvers in actual combat situations, tactical bombardment operations, opforce disruption, the abilities and limits of her weapons systems.

Her body couldn't sleep at computer speeds, but she spent twelve to fifteen hours a day at a subjective rate of 100:1, packing over 15,000 hours of study and simulation into two weeks sidereal.

During this period, Jane monitored the progress of the factory container in fabricating her weapons module and the munitions for it. Three weeks wasn't a lot of time, but she had already had the factory container forging and rolling the required metals before she ever arrived, and it was a large facility. She picked the Guild Weapons Module for Tow Craft Mark 27 (Planetary Engagement Edition) as the best unit for her purposes that could still be ready in time.

Another part of the facility was making modern basic infantry weapons and personal shield generator/communicators in large quantities, as well as drop containers that would connect to the drop rails on the weapons module. The shields would not hold against modern weapons, but they would hold against the hundred-year-old-technology pellet pistols that the GP had.

She sent periodic reports to the Adamant High Command from "Brigadier General Brin Denton". She allowed his explanations -- of why he couldn't get the factory container to the planet quicker, of all the difficulties they were having in loading the software, and in getting the docked ships under way with the tow boat's much more powerful drive -- to become more threadbare as the weeks went on. All tyrants were paranoid because so many people really did want them dead, and it was time to start building suspicion.

She also analyzed the data that came in from the Mark 53 Comm Pack she had dropped earlier. The node had inserted itself into the Guild-designed planetary communications net, and gained access to the Guild-designed computer systems used by the military and the GP. She copied the entire military and GP databases, with the result that she not only knew where their troops were, she also knew where the most stubborn pockets of dissidents and resistance were.

Finally, she prepared update briefings for Captain Dawkins and XO Ferrano, and simulations for the ship's crew. She would be handling the weapons and maneuvering from her pilot's chair, but she wanted them up to date and practiced in maneuvering with the weapons module in case of some emergency or engineering failure.

The third week Jane Henderson spent in sidereal time, to let her body recover from how hard she had been pushing. She had spent over two years subjective time studying, and now there was only one week left.

"My goal is to get them defending against what they think they are facing, and thereby weaken themselves against our attack," Jane Henderson said. Also in the briefing room were Captain Dawkins and XO Ferrano.

"I think I see. If they think it is an internal security issue, they'll button up rather than try to deploy their forces against us," Ferrano said.

"Exactly. If they think Denton is part of an in-house coup attempt, and that some of their own forces are in on it, they will try to keep their forces concentrated where loyalists can keep an eye on everybody. Concentration of their forces helps us by making them easier to kill and reduces collateral damage," Jane said.

"You're going for a massive kill on their forces? You aren't going to try to force a surrender?" Dawkins asked.

"Too many things can go wrong, and most of them involve us taking serious damage or getting killed. Losing Guild personnel or having Guild personnel trapped in the system is not an option. I suppose we could take the station home, but without a pilot's chair I wouldn't want to try it. Our best bet then would be to take the station on a time-dilation loop forward to its next port call and see if a Guild ship shows up. But they won't even know we are missing yet at that point. It could take a hundred years sidereal for word to get back and the Guild to get a ship out here. So it would be pure luck. Not interested," Jane said. "Look, that's a volunteer force. All those people chose to be GP, to support the regime. Yeah, there are going to be a lot of widows and orphans, but we're going to reset the situation on the planet and leave. I don't want to leave a whole bunch of people around who are willing to support this sort of thing, and have experience at it, to get it all going again. They've done us the favor of sorting themselves out from the rest of the population, and I'm going to take advantage of it."

Dawkins nodded. "Why will they think it's Denton playing a double game? Why won't they see through that, guess the truth? I mean, any Guild personnel would know that trip out here was being done by a pilot," he said.

"First, they don't know anything about how Guild ships work. They think they are just like any of the in-system ships we give them. Except we're holding back on the interstellar drive technology, of course." Jane rolled her eyes, and Dawkins and Ferrano smiled. "So Denton and his men, in their eyes, should be able to figure it out. Second, these people believe in force -- numbers of men, kinds of weapons. They had 500 people on that station, and they know we don't have near that number of people, so there's no way we could have overpowered them. Third, the natural paranoia of a fascist regime makes the internal threat more real to them. Fourth, I have been sending some pretty graphic videos ahead with Denton's reports," she said.

Dawkins and Ferrano both raised questioning eyebrows.

"I sent them videos of Denton's people torturing me to get the information on how to program and run the factory container. I pulled torture videos out of their database, then doctored the videos to show them torturing me. I don't have a vagina or an anus, so the rape parts took some creative video editing. But they've seen Denton's people torturing me with their own approved methods, all by the book, and me breaking down and telling them the secrets of how to run the factory container. That was early on, though, and now they have to be wondering what's taking so long," Jane said.

"They have approved methods for torture?" Ferrano asked.

"Oh, yes, including rape, of both men and women. With detailed instructions on how to make it most effective. And a regime that has detailed manuals on how to rape people most effectively to break them down, is not a regime I am going to leave in place," Jane said. She turned to Dawkins. "Nor will I be overly concerned with their casualties. I'm just afraid I'm going to miss some of the bastards."

"And fifth," she continued, "I've got a little trick up my sleeve that ought to stir the hornet's nest up a bit first. If I can cast suspicion on some of the more competent high-level officers -- the ones that can tell their heads from their asses -- I might be able to get them out of commission for a bit, and have the least capable people in place when we actually show up."

Jane Henderson had composed a few cryptic text-only messages from "BD" to his co-conspirators in the non-existent coup. These were dated over the course of the past month. She knew that message traffic was routinely computer scanned by Internal Security, an elite investigations group whose job it was to protect the regime from threats originating inside the government and armed forces. She looked at that program and knew the scan parameters that would surface a troublesome message to a human investigator. She was careful to avoid that in this string of messages.

She inserted those messages into their proper places within the message archive the IS kept on their internal computers, which she had access to on her Senior Guild Pilot authority. IS knew nothing of that hidden super-user login, but it was a Guild-designed computer running Guild-designed software. Those messages showed the addressees as the head of the GP, the assistant head of the army, and several other key players, all of whom, according to their service records, were the most competent in their chains of command. Repressive regimes always feared the competent the most. The incompetent couldn't pull off a coup anyway.

The small space force was a more difficult matter, because the chief of that service and his assistant were both competent. She put the chief of the space forces down as an addressee. She had other plans for the assistant.

Once those messages were in place, she sent a message through the system to the same addressees, cryptically advising that "BD" would be on the way back within two days, with all required items, and that the rendezvous points and times were as previously agreed. Jane composed this message specifically to trigger the scan. "Rendezvous," it seemed, was a flag word.

Investigator Ronn Morton was one of the Internal Security people who looked at messages kicked out by the message scanning software. Tedious duty, but someone had to do it, and a couple of conspiracies had been turned up as a result over the past several years. It was, therefore, a job Internal Security took seriously.

This message was a bit troubling. Not really anything there. Really cryptic, though. Morton ran a back search for messages to the same addressees with the signature "BD". *Well, that is certainly getting interesting,* he thought. Message origin indicated it came in on an RF channel normally used for space forces traffic. He ran a personnel search on government personnel currently in space with the initials BD. *Bingo!*

He keyed his terminal to connect to his superior. When Chief Inspector Eamer, the head of the Internal Security group in charge of message scanning, took the call, Morton first apologized.

"Sorry to interrupt you, Sir, but I think you really should take a look at this as soon as possible."

One of the main factory-bay hatches of the factory container slid open, and a cylinder larger than the *Jane Henderson* floated out of the bay on robot thrusters. It drifted aft along the immense side of the factory container to its rear face, and the robot thrusters then moved it to the #4 docking port. Once in place, it was secured with the docking clamps and the robot thruster units retreated back into the bay and the hatch closed.

Jane Henderson came onto the bridge as the docking maneuver was completing.

The *Jane Henderson*, under XO Ferrano's direction, and using maneuvering thrusters only, had undocked from the station, pulled away from the factory container, hopped over to the new cylinder at #4 docking port, and docked with the new cylinder. As the factory container's thrusters were in front as it decelerated toward the planet, all of this activity took place on the back side of the container from the planet.

Jane walked over to her observer's chair to the left of Chon Dawkins' command chair, on the other side from the XO. Dawkins was watching his XO carry out the maneuvers.

"That's awful big for a Mark 27, Ma'am. It's almost half as big as the station," Dawkins said as Jane took her seat.

"It's just a shell, a hold container. We'll shed it at the last minute," Jane said. "The Mark 27 is the center portion of this end of the container. That's what your XO actually docked to. I want them to think that Denton is on his way back with a big hold container full of whiz-bang weapons for the coup."

"Well, a Mark 27 weapons module is nothing to sneeze at, Ma'am. And you said it has full weapons racks?"

"Yep. All racks full."

"That's an awful lot of firepower, Ma'am. Thirty-six MITREMs, plus all the other stuff?"

The Multiple Independently Targetable Re-Entry Munition was the Central World's current technology for planetary tactical bombardment. Each MITREM contained five hundred 2KTAMBs -- 2 Kilo-Ton Anti-Matter Bomblets. Each bomblet was only a couple of cubic feet in volume, and most of that was guidance and control systems, as well as the superconductor anti-matter containment. You could get a really big bang out of a very small amount of anti-matter. The whole MITREM was under 2000 cubic feet -- a sphere about 16 feet in diameter. Thirty-six MITREMs was a total of 36 Megatons.

"I'll probably only need six. And half of them will be MITREM-Bs."

"Well, we're docked to it now. We can depart as soon as the computers have checked the control links, Ma'am."

"Let's set departure for ten hours from now, Captain. That will give our primary watch shift a night's sleep and a good meal before action. It also will get us into position on the planet when it's full daylight on the most populous continent. We wouldn't want any of our friends down there to be at home in bed and miss all the fun."

Jane Henderson was plugging into her pilot's chair as Chon Dawkins undocked the *Jane Henderson* and the hold container covering the Mark 27 weapons module from the factory container. The deceleration of the factory container held them in place for the moment.

Dawkins turned his captain's chair to face Jane. "We're ready when you are, Ma'am."

"Go ahead and separate us, and get us clear of the factory container, Captain," Jane said. "And warn everyone this could get bumpy."

"Yes, Ma'am." Dawkins turned his chair back around. "OK, let's get some separation, Mr. Warner."

"Yes, Sir. Separating now."

As Jane's clamshell was closing, the ship lifted from the factory container's #4 docking port, then started to crab over to the side to clear the decelerating container.

Jane Henderson activated the five-space viewer and took in the global view. There was the factory container, and the Jane Henderson separating, pulling the Mark 27 and the hold container covering it. Ahead the planet. Now where was the Adamant space forces station? Ah, there it was. She had to time her arrival when it was in exactly the right spot in its orbit. She wanted it to the side of the planet, so she could fly past.

The space forces had obtained their own space station decades back. For one thing, the Guild freight station was only in orbit for a few months every ten years, so this permanently available station gave the planet access to space, a place to service in-system ships and their crews. It was now being used primarily as a terror weapon, as any opponent stupid enough to fight the regime could be bombarded from space by those in-system ships.

The space forces station was a Guild design, delivered as a kit several port calls back. One job that had been on the list for the factory container had been to build and site a larger space station, and increase its complement of ships. In that plan, the existing space station would be surplus, and could be broken down by the factory container for raw materials.

The space station also represented the only in-space threat to the *Jane Henderson*.

Jane had the Mark 53 Comm Pack monitoring the government computers and communications nets, and sending her anything interesting. Lots of arrest orders flying about, and several arrests had already been made, so that part of it was working out so far.

As the *Jane Henderson* cleared the factory container, Captain Dawkins cut the thrusters and let the decelerating factory container fall behind. He flipped the ship end-for-end to bring its engines around as the factory container slid past.

"I have the con, Captain," Jane signaled Dawkins from within the viewer. As with all voice communications when she was in accelerated mode within the computer, she queued it up in a voice synthesizer for real-time delivery.

"You have the con, Ma'am," Dawkins said.

Jane started building the singularity, spinning it up until it was a blazing diamond in front of her. There was no gravity well to worry about this time, and she began accelerating toward the planet. She was hotdogging it a little bit with only the Mark 27 in tow, but not fast enough, she hoped, to alarm the Adamant government. As far as they knew, it was Brin Denton, blissfully unaware that his coup had been discovered, bringing modern weapons to troops loyal to himself and his co-conspirators.

The problem was, it was not fast enough to get her to the speed she wanted for her attack run. She had to take out that space station and its docked in-system ships before they could deploy against her. The Adamant government had made the problem much simpler by "grounding" all the ships on the station, lest they be used in the non-existent coup, and that helped tremendously. As long as they stayed in place, she only had one target.

She waited, letting her velocity build at her current acceleration, and monitored the communications from the planet to the station. Just a little longer before you decide to deploy, just a little more.

Jane reached her pre-planned point, and triggered the sending of another message. She had programmed this message into the Mark 53 Comm Pack, but the node was programmed to kick the message off from the terminal of the assistant head of the space forces. She could see he was at his terminal, so he was in the office. The message was ostensibly from him to Brigadier General Brin Denton: "Hurry! IS on to us!" This message came from, but did not display on, his terminal. Instead, she displayed on his terminal a cryptic message requiring his urgent attendance at a meeting several miles away.

Internal Security arrested him in the parking lot as he ran to his personal vehicle.

Jane now started accelerating in earnest, just as Brin Denton might. She fed energy into the singularity at the tow's maximum feed rate. With only the Mark 27 in tow, the Guild tow ship piled on the gravities.

Ferrano was watching her displays with astonishment. "Wow. Has the *Jane Henderson* ever cut loose like this, Sir?" Ferrano asked Dawkins.

"In the thirty-five ship-time years I've been in command, since this ship was new, I have never seen the Senior Pilot push this hard. Not even close," Dawkins said. *And I hope the ship stays together*, remained unsaid.

Jane wasn't aiming for a zero-velocity meet with the planet. She was well past the normal turnover point when she orbited the ship around in front of the singularity and started decelerating. Carrying this big of a singularity through the planet's gravity well was going to get interesting. Once the ship had flipped, she released the hold container covering the Mark 27 weapons module and let it continue on at its current velocity.

The ship lurched as the hold container separated. That was a first for Chon Dawkins. Then again, the *Jane Henderson* had never undocked from a container during deceleration before, either. He watched the container drop away from the ship.

The hold container continued on at 10,000 kilometers per second. Just three percent of c. But it hit the Adamant space forces' space station like the hammer of God.

The *Jane Henderson* came in right behind it.

Jane was decelerating hard, the large singularity she had built now behind the *Jane Henderson* as the ship bore down on the wreckage of the space station. As she approached the space station, Jane orbited the ship around the singularity so it was toward the planet from the moving singularity. This applied side vector to hold against the planet's pull on the singularity.

It also got the ship out of the way as the singularity hit the spreading wreckage of the space station and the hold container. The Jane Henderson had thousands of gravities of acceleration at the moment, and it was miles away from the singularity. The huge gravitational stresses on the wreckage, that close to the singularity as it passed directly through the debris, disintegrated the wreckage and left behind only a cloud.

The ship lurched again, harder, as the singularity passed through the space station.

"Holy sh-- The singularity vaporized the station," Ferrano said.

"Actually, it ate some of it. That's why the lurch. Our acceleration increased when the singularity took in the extra energy. We were moving too fast for it to swallow most of it. But, yes, that was the most thorough demolition of a space habitat I have ever seen -- or ever want to," Dawkins said.

Jane orbited the *Jane Henderson* back to the front of the singularity and continued decelerating hard as they shot past the planet. She was pulling energy out of the singularity and ejecting relativistic streams of condensed matter from the rear of the ship in a ring of jets around the Mark 27. The gravities shot even higher, and her speed relative to the planet was coming down rapidly.

The ride got pretty rough as the ship shook at the center of the maelstrom of forces.

"She's using the energy bleeds as additional deceleration," Ferrano said.

"Well, she has to get rid of the extra energy she picked up from the station debris somehow. We can't store it all. But look at those acceleration numbers. She's right at the edge of the tested performance envelope of the ship.," Dawkins said. "Still holding together, but make sure those damage control parties are ready down in engineering in case things start coming apart."

The ship stopped relative to the planet and started picking up speed back toward it at the same dizzying acceleration. Jane continued to pull mass out of the singularity, sending some of it back into her stores and continuing to vent the excess to the rear. The gravities started dropping even as the velocity continued to increase. She needed the velocity to close with the planet again after her fast overflight, but she had to be able to decelerate again to get a near-zero-velocity meet with the planet.

"People of Adamant. The Pilots Guild is not your enemy. The tyrant Shluter and his cronies are your enemy. The General Police is your enemy. The space forces are your enemy. The corrupt army is your enemy. But that is past, for the day you have dreamed of has come. Your freedom is at hand. The Guild ship *Jane Henderson* has just destroyed the space forces' space station, and is even now beginning the destruction of the tyrant Shluter's forces on the planet. We are also dropping infantry weapons and shields to the resistance forces.

"Resistance forces, your individual terminals and communications devices will tell you when and where to obtain these weapons, and how to use them. We will destroy the main forces and resources of the enemy. It is up to you to do the rest.

"Senior Guild Pilot Jane Henderson out."

The Mark 53 Comm Pack had spent weeks characterizing each and every communications device on the planetary communications net, with the result that this message was broadcast over every terminal, every handheld communications device, every entertainment and computational system on the planet, except those used by government agencies and government forces. There followed individualized messages to 200,000 people whom the Mark 53 Comm Pack had identified as resistance members, detailing the landing spot and time of the weapons container that person should head for, and containing a brief tutorial.

Most of their training would have to be by doing.

The Mark 53 Comm Pack now also began the systematic disruption of the government's communications resources. Any attempts to communicate with the populace, to claim that in fact the Guild was attacking Adamant to enslave the planet, as they had claimed all along, were blocked. Any communications to government forces to deploy against the threat were blocked. But any communications to government forces calling them to barracks, or any other communication that would concentrate forces, went through without any problem.

And all the media were blocked. All of them were in the pocket of the government anyway. Instead, all media sources continued to repeat Jane Henderson's message.

As the *Jane Henderson* decelerated on its approach to the planet, Jane Henderson checked all her targeting parameters. She was good for the tactical bombardment. And the Mark 53 Comm Pack was keeping track of the whereabouts of Marc Shluter. After the space station was destroyed, he retreated to the bunker deep under his capital. She had allocated three bomblets, set for contact, and added a fourth for luck.

The Mark 27 weapons module was an exposed frame design. It looked like a packed cargo bay that someone had forgotten to skin over. The spherical MITREMs were racked down the central core of the Mark 27, six MITREMs in each circle, six circles deep, and each circled rotated 30 degrees from its neighbors so they would pack more densely.

Jane tracked her velocity closely, and at the precisely plotted moment, ejected one circle of six MITREMs from the rear of the *Jane Henderson*. As she was decelerating, the singularity was behind her, and the Mark 27 in front. She watched in her display as the

MITREMs continued on toward the planet, then ejected two circles of six MITREM-Bs.

Next up were the infantry weapons containers. The external framework of the Mark 27 weapons module was covered with racks that could be used for deploying mines, infantry support packs with rations, water, and such, and, as in this case, infantry weapons packs. Each infantry weapons pack contained one hundred GPIRX (General Purpose Infantry Rifle Mark 10) rifles. These were energy rifles where the charge could be dialed in for the specific use: anti-personnel, anti-vehicle, anti-armor, even demolition. Range settings could be set for "no-closer-than" and "no-farther-than". There was even a mortar mode.

With each rifle, there was also a personal shield/communicator. The device was worn like a vest, and included a small shield generator the size of one's hand both front and rear. It would protect the wearer's torso and head against the explosive pellets of the government's arms, though not against the modern GPIRX rifles. The unit also included voice communications, as well as forward-facing video.

There were 2000 infantry weapons packs racked in the Mark 27's 40 mine-laying rails.

The infantry weapons packs had a one-drop anti-grav capability, and were individually targetable. Jane had chosen 2000 muster points in and near the major pockets of the resistance by the simple expedient of mapping their communications devices.

When the *Jane Henderson* hit the deployment point, still decelerating, Jane unlocked the rails, and 40 trains of 50 infantry weapons packs each rolled down the rails and fell ahead of the ship.

The MITREMs went into orbit about the planet as the infantry weapons packs descended to the surface. Jane had selected one of the resistance members as the company leader for each weapons location, and the weapons pack at each location would only open with the password she had sent to the company commander. A few of the weapons packs were taken by government forces who just happened to be in the locale when they came down. They were quickly subdued by the resistance, who had shown up with what arms they had.

As the arms were being distributed, the MITREMs in orbit disgorged the 2KTAMBs. Three thousand bomblets -- 6 megatons of ordnance -- began their drop to the planet. As they hit atmosphere, they deployed steering and braking flaps behind, looking for all the world like big, metal badminton shuttlecocks.

In any organization like the Adamant resistance, some people will be government agents, trying to get deeper into the organization so that the government can roll up big sections of it at once. Given the fascist government's fascination with keeping track of everyone and everything, they also kept track of who their agents were. The government knew who their agents were, and so did Jane.

She considered not sending the mustering messages to the government agents within the resistance, but the danger was that they would show up anyway as resistance members contacted each other. So instead she gave the names of the government agents who would show up at a given weapons pack to all of the other resistance members detailed to that company.

Most did not last long.

The 2KTAMBs were set to detonate primarily at one of two altitudes: 900 feet for a maximum destruction radius of about three-quarters of a mile, or on contact for minimum destruction radius of about one-half mile. For this calculation Jane used the radius of a 10 PSI over-pressure in the shock wave. This would flatten most buildings and cause death to exposed personnel. Lesser damage all the way down to broken windows would carry out a lot further.

The targets were military bases, barracks, and government centers, including the headquarters buildings for the government military services and the presidential complex. Larger facilities took two or three or even four of the K2TAMBs, spread out to cover the required area.

Four K2TAMBs went in on the presidential palace with its deep underground bunker, at three-minute intervals. These exploded on contact, gouging out a deeper and deeper crater into which the subsequent ones fell. The crater concentrated the explosive effect by constraining the lateral shock wave.

Jane was watching the terminal traffic and the video monitors within the bunker. Marc Shluter was there, right up until Jane lost contact. Exterior view from a rooftop weather camera a mile away indicated that the bunker was breached on the third hit. The fourth hit shot large pieces of the concrete bunker up into the air.

The K2TAMB is a small weapon as nuclear explosives go, but a one-mile-diameter zone of destruction is still a pretty big spot on the map. There were facilities that Jane simply could not go after with nukes. The collateral damage to hitting a police building in a large city was unacceptable. This is what the MITREM-Bs were for.

The Multiple Independently Targetable Re-Entry Munition - Ballistic was in every way the same as the MITREM, except without the warheads. Each MITREM-B contained five hundred NEBBs, Non-Explosive Ballistic Bomblets. The NEBBs had the same steering and braking flaps, and the same guidance systems, as the 2KTAMBs, but instead of the two kiloton anti-matter warhead, the NEBBs had one cubic foot of solid iron, organized as ten equal-mass pellets. A 780-pound, 20-inch-diameter projectile falling through atmosphere will reach a terminal velocity of 530 miles per hour.

As the 2KTAMBs were on final acquisition of their targets, the twelve MITREM-Bs disgorged the NEBBs. Six thousand more bomblets began their drop to the planet. They deployed their steering and braking flaps as they hit atmosphere, targeting smaller government facilities, or those closer to civilian populations: police buildings in cities, guard barracks in concentration camps, and local offices of government agencies, like its media and propaganda offices.

Five minutes after the nuclear bombardment of the major facilities, minor facilities were being destroyed around the planet. Each NEBB came screaming down out of the sky, split apart a hundred feet from the target to maximize damage, and passed straight through the building, from the top down. The building imploded in behind it.

Jane used the Mark 53 Comm Pack to monitor communications, especially communications between and among survivors of the regime. She then transmitted deployment orders to her 2000 company commanders, sending them to seize points of control and communication, to clear areas of surviving GP, and to liberate concentration camps.

There were a couple of areas where surviving regime members got organized enough to offer resistance, but they found that their guns were ineffective against resistance members wearing the personal shields, while they were defenseless against the GPIRX rifles.

It was all over pretty quickly.

Based on the government's computer records, there were several surviving members of prior planetary governments alive, usually in concentration camps. She instructed the resistance companies liberating those camps, in addition to feeding and taking care of the medical needs of the inmates, to find them. She needed a cadre of political types with some legitimacy around which to form a transitional government.

That done, Jane Henderson exited the five-space viewer and opened the clamshell. Her attendants assisted her with disconnecting her tubing and helped her to the wheelchair. She had not been in the pilot's chair long -- just a couple of days -- but she had spent most of that at 50:1 and was on the edge of exhaustion.

Dawkins was there. "Nicely done, Ma'am."

"We got lucky. So much could have gone wrong. I had contingency plans on top of contingency plans, and I didn't need any of them. And the ruse worked longer than I thought it possibly could. Even so, I probably just killed several million people."

"And freed hundreds of times as many. Don't forget that, Ma'am. Don't ever forget that."

Jane Henderson was conversing over a video link with the president of the transitional government. He had been a popular vice president of the pre-Shluter government twenty years ago. To the shell-shocked public, he was a symbol of the past, a remnant of a better time. He had a name, but everyone just called him "The Old Man." He was already looking much healthier now, more than a month after the destruction of the Shluter government, than he had on being found in one of the concentration camps.

The GPIRX rifles and personal shields had been rendered inoperative by a command that had set them to fuse their control circuitry. The factory container was once more out among the asteroids, building the new, replacement, space station for Adamant, along with a fleet of new, more capable, in-system ships. The Guild freight station had departed on its next ten-year time-dilation loop, Berwick and Bannon in command. The *Jane Henderson* was preparing for departure, a loaded Guild freight container in tow.

"Are you making progress in your planning, Mr. President?" Jane asked.

"Oh, yes. It will be a parliamentary system. The parliament can maintain tighter control over the executive, as the prime minister can be removed by a no-confidence vote. Hopefully that will avoid a future repetition of this whole sad state of affairs. Our head of state will be the oldest living former prime minister. To start off with, there has been an effort to draft me for that position, and I haven't ruled it out. It's a ceremonial role, but symbolically important for all that. We've been submitting these questions to the public through the comm net, and the Mark 53 comm node you've left with us is ensuring that people don't cheat on the voting. Thank you for that, Madam Pilot."

"Glad to help, Mr. President. And thank you for expediting getting a cargo together for us on our next hop."

"The least we could do after all you have done for us. Even so, I do have two questions for you."

"Go ahead," Jane asked.

"We would like to honor you in some way. A parade, perhaps, so the people of Adamant can see who rescued them. I am aware that you are using an avatar on this link, which I don't mind at all, but people are very curious about you. You have become an important figure in our history, Madam Pilot."

"I'm afraid I don't make planetary landings, Mr. President. I can count on one hand the number of times I have even been off my ship in the last four hundred years. I'm sorry."

"Ah. Well, could we perhaps have a 3-D image of you -- the real you, not the avatar?"

Jane thought about that, and figured why not? "Certainly, Mr. President. I can do that."

"Excellent. The other question I had for you is to ask some advice. What sort of monument should we erect to remind people of this episode in our history? What do you think would best serve as a warning to the future? I am at something of a loss, and I wondered if you had any ideas, Madam Pilot."

"Interesting question, Mr. President." Jane thought for a moment. "How about leaving the crater where the presidential palace once stood? A symbol of the destruction the regime wreaked upon the people of Adamant. Perhaps mark it with a plaque or something."

"An excellent idea, Madam Pilot. I will give it further thought." The Old Man considered for a moment. "Any ideas about what the plaque should say?"

Jane Henderson started building the singularity, spinning it up until it was a blazing diamond in front of her. Slowly she moved away from the planet. As she gained distance from the planet's gravity well, she fed more power into the singularity, increased the pace of her acceleration. After over two months ship-time in the Adamant system, and almost two-and-a-half years of subjective time, she exulted in flying once more among the stars. She was home again at last.

A hundred years after the Shluter Tyranny, the parliamentary republic of Adamant still stands, is stronger, in fact, than ever. The colony is thriving, growing, building a better future for its citizens.

The presidential palace stands to the west of a half-mile-wide crater in the center of the planet's capital, the prime minister's residence stands to the east of the crater, and the massive parliament building stands to the south.

North of the crater, on a fifty-foot pedestal, stands a fifty-foot bronze statue of a Senior Guild Pilot, clad in a simple shipsuit, symbiont on her head and life-support connections at her throat. The statue points down into the center of the crater. In three-foot high letters on its base reads the inscription:

HERE DIED

MARC SHLUTER

THAT BASTARD

It's About T.I.M.E.

The Tree

I dropped over to Billy's one Saturday several years back to see what he was up to. He lives in a wooded valley a couple miles out of town and I normally stop by a couple times a month when I happen by. I pulled up in the yard and he was out tinkering with his old pickup, a half-ton Chevy from the 1970's.

"Hey, there, Billy. Whaddya call a sixty-year-old redneck?"

"Lucky. That's an old one, Red. Hey, give me a hand with this topper, will ya? I got it off myself, but it'll be a bear to get it back on without a hand."

"Sure."

As we were getting ready to put the topper back on, I checked out what was in the bed. Billy's pickup was normally full of miscellaneous bits of miscellaneous machinery -- what other people would call junk -- but not today. There was a tangle of cables and tubing connecting several pieces of -- something. It looked like some sort of lab apparatus. All of it in machined brass and stainless steel, obviously a one-off. And it was bolted down to the bed floor, a semi-permanent installation.

"Whatcha got there, Billy?"

"Oh, this here's a time machine."

"Uh, Billy. Did you skip the rails, buddy? That whole 'build a time machine in your garage' thing? You think I was born yesterday?"

"No, no, I didn't build it. Not by myself anyway. This here's from NASA."

Billy worked at NASA in Huntsville, about 30 miles down the road, over in the next county. For all his country-boy ways, Billy was a top machinist, a tool and die maker actually. Holding tolerances of a couple ten-thousandths of an inch was no big deal for him. And what he couldn't machine up couldn't be built.

"You stole a time machine from NASA?"

"Nah. Budget cuts. We been working on this thing for a couple years, and then one day they just up and cancels the project. So they tell me to junk it. I couldn't just throw it out, now could I?"

"So you're mounting it in your pickup truck."

"Where else?"

"So what's it do?"

"Well, I'm not completely up on the theory of it, but I picked up some things. You know, an object at rest will stay at rest, right?"

"Yeah, momentum and inertia and all that."

"Right. So think of a beer sittin' on the picnic table. Nobody messes with it, it's just gonna sit there. And if you move the table, the beer goes with it. Well, that's sorta the way time works. We all just sit there in time, but time itself is moving, and we get carried along."

"OK, I got that. So what does the machine do?"

"Well, it creates a time bubble. It sorta disconnects the beer from the table. Now the beer can move around. Not sure how the moving part works, but we did some testing on it, and it seems to work fine."

"So you can travel in time? Go anywhere -- I guess I should say anywhen -- you want?"

"Well, yes and no. You can make the time bubble go back and forth, but you can't leave the bubble until you're back in your own present."

"What would happen if you tried?"

"The theory boys didn't know for sure, but all the alternatives were bad."

"How bad?"

"Well, it seemed the only thing they weren't sure about was how big the explosion would be. That's one of the reasons they canceled the project. Since you can't get out, they said it wasn't useful."

"Wasn't useful? Are you kidding? Are they all morons?"

"Well, there's a lot of bright people at NASA, Red. Scientists and such. But the management types, well, it's sorta hit or miss."

We got the topper on the back, being careful not to hit the machine, then Billy motioned me to get in the truck. He and I climbed in, and I saw there was an extra lever sticking up out of the floor next to the four-wheel-drive selector.

"So, you wanna try it out?"

"Billy, are you sure this is safe?"

"Nope. Not sure anyway. But nothing bad happened to the test cat."

"Test cat?"

"Yeah, we built a little mechanism to run the controls. It ran the machine backwards two days, waited five minutes, and then ran it back. The cat was fine."

"So what was it like? Did it disappear or something?"

"Nope, just sat there. It came back to the same time it left. Didn't see anything at all."

"Then how do you know it worked?"

"The cat was wearing a watch around its neck. The watch was off by exactly five minutes. And the internal camera recorded two days of us running around the lab, first in reverse, then in forward."

Billy grinned at me and started the engine.

"Engine needs to be running. Gotta get power for the thing from somewhere."

When the idle had settled down, Billy flipped a switch on the dash. After a couple of seconds, there was a barely audible hum.

"So, Red, forward, or back?"

"Forward. I already saw yesterday."

Billy laughed and reached for the control. He pulled it to the left, then pushed it forward just a bit, and what we saw out of the windows got just a little misty, as if seen through a slight haze. We watched the sun arc across the sky, set, and then after a few minutes, rise again.

"Well, don't that beat all. Give it some more juice, Billy."

Billy advanced the control, and the view turned stroboscopic, as the sun rose and set, rose and set, faster and faster. The leaves on the trees all turned color, fell, and we were into winter. Then the spring came and all the leaves grew back. Suddenly the view changed. Billy pulled the control back to neutral and we stopped. A tree on the edge of the woods lay fallen across his mobile home, which was pretty smashed up.

"Damn. Maggie's been nagging me to get that tree down before it fell down. I guess I better get that done."

He stared at the tree that smashed his house for a bit, shook his head.

"Well, let's head back, make sure we can reverse the process."

Billy pulled the lever back, and we started going back in time.

"How do we know when we get to the right time?"

"Oh, we're still anchored in our present. It will stop when we get back. To go backward, I have to switch modes."

As we neared the correct time, the process slowed a bit, and then stopped. Billy put the lever back in the center position, shut off the engine. We got out, and I just stared at the truck, sitting there like nothing had happened. Billy was looking off at that tree. He sighed and started for the pole barn.

"Where you headed, Billy?"

"To get the ankle spikes and the chain saw. I gotta get that damn tree down. C'mon, Red. Give me a hand."

The Stock Market

As we were cleaning up the debris from the tree, I thought about Billy's time machine.

The discarded NASA device he had mounted in the bed of his old pickup truck had taken us forward in time to where we could see that the tree would fall on his house next spring, presumably in a spring storm of the kind we got pretty often here in central Alabama. When we returned to the present and took the tree down, we saw just how hollowed out and weak it was, which was not apparent just from looking at it. So that seemed to check.

But the implications of a machine like this just kept occurring to me as we worked. What if you could go ahead and see what the future was, or, at least, would be if you didn't modify it? You could take steps now, like us cutting down this tree, to make sure that future, the unmolested one, did not take place. And it would play hell with futures markets. Hmm.

"Billy, does anyone else know about this device? That you have it, I mean?"

"Other 'n you and me? Nope. It's one of them Swiss Navy projects."

"Switzerland doesn't have a navy."

"Exactly."

"Got it. OK, so I think we might want to keep it quiet. Just between the two of us."

"That seems reasonable to me. I don't want to have to be giving people rides and stuff. And the government types might get a little frisky about just how I ended up with it."

"Exactly. But there's a couple other reasons. Billy, you're coming up on 60 years old, same as me. How are you and Maggie fixed for retirement?"

"Oh, we got my pension, and both of us will have Social Security and Medicare. We'll be all right."

"How about an extra million or five? Would that come in handy?"

"Well, sure. Not sure what all we would do with that much money, but a little extra never hurts. Whatcha got in mind?"

"Well, if you know the future, you can put your money into things you know are going to do really well, but that other people don't know about."

"Like betting on the horses?"

"Like that, but if you call the trifecta at Hialeah every day for a week, people are going to get suspicious. I was thinking more of the stock market. If you saw in the future that some company was going to make it big, you could come back here and buy stock in it cheap. You can make even more money by betting against some company that you knew was going to fail. And making a couple of investments in the market that pay off big is much less likely to draw attention."

"Wouldn't that be cheatin'?"

"Well, I suppose, but I don't know of any rules against it. The stock market's got all kinds of rules, but I don't think they covered the time machine angle."

"Well, if there ain't no rules against it, it ain't cheatin'."

"A very enlightened attitude. Why don't we take a trip into town for a bit?"

We drove into town, stopping on the way at my place so I could pick up my wife's camera and the big telephoto lens she used when birdwatching.

"OK, Billy, now what we need is a newspaper box that has the Wall Street Journal."

"Well, I'm not sure which papers they have, but there's a bunch of paper boxes in front of the diner downtown."

"Can you see them from the street? Somewhere where you can have the boxes right outside my window?"

"Yeah, I think so. Let's go look."

So we headed downtown, and the Journal did in fact have a box outside the diner. It was facing the street, too, but that street was one way the wrong way, and the parking lane stopped a ways back. We would be right in the middle of the oncoming left-hand turn lane.

"Well, that won't work."

"Why not?"

Billy flipped the switch on the dash to turn on the time machine, and then swung the truck into the one-way street the wrong way, facing up the left-hand turn lane. He immediately pulled the time lever he had installed on the floor to the left and the world once again became a little hazy, the sign we were in the time bubble.

"No problem."

"OK, good. Now what we want to do is to go forward a week or so at a time, and I take a picture of the "Markets" section of the "What's News" column on the front page of the Journal. I can only see the top half of the column through the window, but that should be enough to give us what we need."

I got the big lens on the camera and started working on the focus and framing the shot. When I was ready, I looked up and saw a big truck bear down on us and swing into the left-hand turn lane. I grabbed at the door handle to bail out, but the door wouldn't budge. The big truck hit us head-on -- and passed right through us.

"What the hell?"

"We're not really here, Red. We're in the time bubble. They can't see us, we can only see them."

"Damn, that was scary. A little heads up would be good on stuff like that, Billy. OK, let's go forward a week and start taking pictures."

So Billy pushed the time lever forward and the sun arced across the sky and set, then rose again a few seconds later. He counted days, then stopped, and I snapped a picture. Again and again, we repeated that sequence, until we had gone two years or so into the future.

"OK, that's about two years, Billy. Let's head on back."

Billy set the time control into reverse, and pulled it way back. The sun strobed across the sky, then slowed down, finally stopped.

"OK, Billy, let's get out of here before that truck gets here."

As he backed around the corner, I looked at my watch and groaned. Where had the time gone?

"Look at the time. Sue is going to kill me. She was cooking big tonight, it being Saturday and all."

Billy laughed. "Ain't no time passed at all while we was takin' pictures, Red. Your watch was with us is all. Look at the courthouse clock."

Sure enough, no time had passed while we had spent subjective hours taking pictures.

"Boy, this time machine business takes some getting used to, Billy. I forgot all about that."

Billy drove me back to his place to pick up my car. I was surprised when I got out of the truck that the door opened with no problem at all. I asked Billy about it.

"Well, I think the time bubble field held the truck intact, wouldn't let you open the door. Which is just as well, because if the theory boys are right, you probably would have left a crater where downtown is."

"Really?"

"Yeah, they were all pretty much agreed, except for that one fellow."

"He didn't think it would be a problem?"

"No, he thought it would probably wipe out the whole state. See you later, Red."

The Minister

"Well, Billy, that worked out pretty good."

It was about six months after our time trip to photograph the next two years of the Wall Street Journal front page at the diner downtown. We had made some investments, and they had worked out really well. We were now sitting on the back deck of Billy's new mobile home, that he had set up on the other side of the pole barn from the old one.

"Yeah, Maggie's always wanted a double-wide."

"But you kept the single-wide."

"Yeah, that there's the guest house now. For when the kids 'n grandkids visit."

While we were out on the deck smoking cigars, Maggie and Sue were inside fixing dinner. We never did tell them about the time

109

machine. I had handled our investments through my brother up north, who had been a stock broker for years, setting up joint accounts for both Billy and Maggie, and Sue and I. My brother thought I had developed a hitherto unknown genius for investing, or maybe Billy had. Maggie and Sue, skeptical at first, now thought my brother was an investment genius. Billy and I just kept quiet, let everybody keep whatever misconceptions they had invented to cover the extraordinary circumstances.

Billy and I had each made about two million dollars in six months, and it showed no sign of slowing down. If anything, it was speeding up.

"Well, what are we going to do with the machine now, Billy? I guess we could go sightseeing. You know, go watch the attack on Pearl Harbor or something."

"Nah, we'd have to ship the truck to Hawaii first. Don't forget, you can't move around when you're in the time bubble. There's no friction to push against anything to get you moving. And no brakes. You gotta be where you wanna be when you start. About the only thing exciting we could do around here is go back a hundred, hundred twenty years and watch them build the courthouse."

"Huh. Guess you're right. Well, we'll think of something."

"Tell you what. I got an idea that way. See this here?"

He held up the front section of the local paper, the headline about the terrorist bombing back east.

"I wish I had known about this ahead of time, so's I coulda gone out there and capped those two bastards beforehand."

The next day, we were in the office of the Reverend James Moore.

"Thanks for meeting with us, preacher."

"No problem, Mr. Green. I always enjoy meeting with parishioners, particularly the ones I don't see very often."

Billy blushed a bit, then gestured in my direction.

"This here's my friend, Fred Martin. Everybody calls him Red."

The preacher looked at my red hair and beard, going gray now, and said, "So I see."

"We had what you might call a hypothetical question for you. An ethical question."

"All right. And that would be...?"

"Preacher, let's say you knew somebody was going to do something terrible. Something like this." Billy held up the paper from yesterday. "Would it be wrong to go and cap that basta-- uh, excuse me, to go and kill that fellow before he did it?"

"A difficult question. First, you can't know someone is going to do something ahead of time."

I stepped in here. "Let's say for the moment that you could know, reverend. Not guess, know. Absolutely know."

"Well, I don't know how you could know for sure without some sort of time machine." The preacher smiled at his joke and Billy's expression sort of congealed. "But, even if you did know, how do you know that killing this person ahead of time would solve the problem?"

"How do you mean?"

"What if he were part of a group, and the least militant of the group? He's been holding them back from doing something even more terrible, and by killing him, you've unleashed them to commit an even more heinous act. Or he could be the least competent bomb-maker in the group; the alternate might be able to fashion an even deadlier device. You don't really know what your act of murder -- and it would be murder -- would accomplish. You could make things worse."

"Huh. Preacher, that is something I had not thought of. Let me put you in this position, then. What would you do?"

"One thing would be to contact the authorities, tell them what you suspected." Reverend Moore nodded toward me. "Or knew."

"But let's say they found him with bomb materials, and terrorist literature and all that. The whole nine yards. Then there'd be all kinds of questions about how I knew. Cops'd think I was a part of it or something."

Reverend Moore looked at Billy for a few seconds. "I see. I guess another thing you could do is tell your minister, which is in confidence, then have him relay the information to another minister closer to the scene, have that minister call in the information. And simply refuse to disclose where it came from." He looked off into the distance for a few seconds. "Come to think of it, that gives me another idea. The local minister could do a little asking around, a little snooping. If it is something like a disturbed individual, like in some of these mass shootings, he might be able to intervene in some other way. Some of those people are mentally ill, and need help more than incarceration. But in any case, if he did a little snooping around first, the authorities might think he stumbled on the information in the performance of his pastoral duties."

Billy looked at me, and I thought about it. It seemed like it could work. I nodded to Billy, and he turned back to Reverend Moore.

"OK, preacher. I think your idea could work. So, you 'in'?"

"In? In what? I thought this was a hypothetical question."

So that's how Billy and I caused the Reverend James Moore to found a new ministry, the Temporal Intervention Ministry of Ecumenicals, or TIME.

We asked Reverend Moore if he didn't think that was just a wee bit obvious, and he smiled and said, "You think anybody hearing or reading that is going to say, 'Oh my gosh, they invented a time machine!' Really?"

The Setup

With our deal with the Reverend Moore to work the information we would bring back from the future, Billy and I needed better information. We had been photographing newspapers in the paper boxes in front of the diner, but there were obvious limits to that. In particular, only the top half of the front page showed.

"You know, Billy, we need an easier way to gather information than photographing the newspaper box from the street."

"Yeah, I been thinkin' about that, and I have a guy coming over to set it up. You know Chick, right? Can you hang around for a bit?"

"Sure."

"Meantime, I got somethin' to show you."

Billy led the way to the pole barn and we went in the man door. Billy's old pickup was parked in there, but the time machine was out of sight under the topper. He opened the back hatch of the topper and I saw, across the back of the bed, a wooden box containing no less than a dozen deep-cycle marine batteries.

"Holy smokes, Billy. What you got there?"

"Well, this way we don't have to run the engine when we're in the time bubble. For one thing, I got no idea where the air for the engine comes from, or where the exhaust goes."

"Ouch. I didn't think about that."

"Yeah, I'm surprised we didn't gas ourselves to death with that little trip we took. Maybe air does go back and forth. That could be where that haze comes from. The other thing is, though, you ever thought what if we run out of gas and the time bubble lost power? Hmm?"

Billy looked at me and raised his eyebrows, then laughed at the expression on my face.

"Anyway, now we got plenty of power to go whenever we want and still be sure of getting home."

Chick showed up. He had a technology business in town, setting up computers and TVs and stereos and such. He pulled his van into the yard. Billy closed the topper hatch and went over to the man door to greet him.

"Hey, there, Billy. I got all the stuff you wanted, I think. You gonna show me where to set it up?"

"Yeah, c'mon, Chick. It's in here."

Chick came in and Billy led him over by the truck.

"So what I want is a big monitor set up in front of the windshield on each side, about there and there. Should fill up the whole windshield. You can put them on this shelf here." Billy indicated a shelf he had built across the hood right in front of the windshield, and which cleared the hood of the truck by a scant inch.

"You want monitors right there in front of the windshield?"

"Yeah, so when I park in here I can read the monitors right through the windshield."

"What in hell you want that for?"

"Well, say it's rainin', and Maggie and I was set on the drive-in. What's it to ya, anyway, Chick? That's where I want 'em."

"OK, OK, Billy, no reason to get hot about it. And the other two monitors?"

"I want them set up on these wing shelves here, and over there." Billy indicated a shelf that was on a pivot, and as he did, he swung it over so it was right alongside the truck, and right outside the driver's window. The other one was over by the passenger window.

"Gonna watch two movies at once? I don't get it, Billy. You gonna come out here and set in the truck, with two computer monitors in front of you and one in each side window?"

"Yup. Truck's got the most comfortable seats in the whole house, what with those buckets I put in it. So that's what I want. You gonna do it or not?"

"Sure, sure, Billy, don't get riled. Now you said you want all of these hooked to one computer? All four monitors?"

"Yup. and I want the keyboard, mouse and computer over there on that fixed shelf."

"All the way over there? How you gonna use 'em when you're sittin' in the truck?" That got a sharp look from Billy. "All right, all right. Speakers?"

Billy looked over at me and I barely shook my head. Couldn't see the sense of sound. You couldn't hear anything within the time bubble anyway.

"Nah, we'll just read the subtitles."

Again Chick looked like he was going to object, but a sharp look from Billy and Chick decided not to say anything about it.

"OK, now you want an Internet connection out here on this computer? You got a good Internet connection in the house I can run over?"

"No, I want it separate. The one in the house ain't fast enough. That's why I want a cell repeater. Mount the directional antenna on that pole out there, and run the cable down the guy wire, and put the repeater antenna in here. You can aim it at that big cell tower a couple ridges over, toward town. Then we'll use the cellular modem in here on the computer."

Chick looked around, sizing it all up. "All right, looks do-able enough, though it beats hell out of me why you want it set up like that." Billy looked like he was getting ready to hit him. "But, hey, it's your money, right? Whatever you want, Billy."

So Billy and I went back out and sat on the front deck and smoked cigars while Chick got everything set up. It was several hours before he was finished. When he was, he called us over to see his handiwork.

The cell repeater, the computer, the monitors were all set up the way Billy wanted them. Billy motioned me to get in the truck, and we both got in and, through the open windows, pulled the wing monitors into place. We were surrounded by computer screens. It was perfect. Billy swung his wing monitor out of the way of the door and got out.

"OK, Chick, that's perfect. What do I owe ya?"

Chick gave him a number, and Billy pulled a big wad out of his pocket and pulled hundreds off of it until Chick was happy. Chick left, and once he was gone Billy pulled a CD out of his pocket.

"Whatcha got there, Billy?"

"I had my grandson set me up some software for this thing. Wait'll you see this."

Billy loaded the software, then installed and ran the program. The four monitors came up with the New York Times website, the Wall Street Journal website, the Fox News website, and the CNN website. As I watched, they started on the home page, then selected each major article one at a time, scrolled to the end of the article, then on to the next article, then finally back to the home page.

"Hey, that's pretty slick there, Billy."

"Yeah, he's a smart kid. Didn't argue with me either. Just crazy grandpa and his latest contraption. So what do you think? New York Times and Wall Street Journal on the windshield monitors, and Fox and CNN on the sides?"

"Sounds good. Who gets which, though?"

So Billy and I played rock-paper-scissors twice. I got stuck with the New York Times on my side of the windshield, but he got CNN in his side monitor, so it balanced out. Billy rearranged the monitors' assignments in Windows and we were all set. We climbed in the truck, swung the wing shelves in toward the truck, and wound the windows up. It was perfect, the news streaming past on all four sides of us. They scrolled pretty fast, but in the time bubble it wouldn't matter, because we could stop at any specific instant.

"So, Red, should we give it a spin?"

The Mall Shooter

Billy and I and Reverend James Moore were sitting on Billy's deck, talking about what to do next. We had shown Jim the time machine, as well as the information we had on the mall shooting that was the first item on our list of events we wanted to stop. A mentally disturbed young man would enter a large shopping mall in Minneapolis and kill 43 men, women, and children on the Saturday before Christmas, two weeks from now.

"So the police didn't believe your guy in Minneapolis, Jim?"

"That's right, Billy. We have a TIME contact in the Minneapolis clergy, and he approached the police about the upcoming event. They told him he couldn't know the future, and besides the mall had pretty good security already."

"But this nutball has it all planned out. He's gonna stand at one of the entrances and shoot half a dozen rounds of subsonic into the interior of the mall, breaking windows and causing panic, and then when security runs toward the center of the mall where they think the problem is, the crowd's gonna be running for the exits, right toward him."

I added, "By the time the people in front figure out what's going on, the rest of the crowd behind them is still going to be headed to the exit, blocking their retreat. That's why the death toll is so high. And the mall is a gun-free zone on top of it."

"Yes, yes, I know, Red. But my contact in Minneapolis has an alternate plan."

Reverend Moore had done a tremendous job recruiting clergy for the Temporal Intervention Ministry of Ecumenicals, or TIME, concentrating on those cities where there would be incidents while we sorted out all the detailed data we needed from the news websites we recorded with Sue's camera while we were in the time bubble. Apparently he had a good contact in Minneapolis. I sure hoped so.

Reverend Paul Whitely looked around at the seven other ministers who had gathered in his office.

"You've all taken the NRA Basic Pistol Class by now?"

Nods all around.

"And you've all obtained your Concealed Carry License?"

Nods again.

"And you have all obtained the recommended weapon and holster, and are carrying it to get comfortable with it?"

More nods. A couple of the ministers pulled their jackets open to reveal Glock model 22 pistols, chambered in .40 Smith & Wesson, in belt holsters located left of center for cross draw.

"Are we going to actually have to shoot him, Paul?" That was Reverend William Michaels.

"I don't know, Bill. Hopefully, he'll surrender to us. But I don't know. If he decides to shoot instead, we'll have to kill him. The only thing I know for sure is what will happen if we don't stop him. We have to protect the innocents in the mall. And if the shooting starts, there's a good chance some of us will go down as well. The best way to limit the carnage is for us to be in practice, so it's off to the range now."

Reverend Whitely led them out to the church van, and they headed off to the indoor range at the local gun store for the first of several planned sessions of target practice. The gun store employees were a little startled to see eight members of the local clergy engaged in deadly earnest practice with silhouette targets, but no one said anything to them.

As Mark Summers walked toward the mall entrance, his pulse was racing. He tried to walk normally, but loaded down with weapons and magazines, it was difficult. There was a big crowd today, lots of people coming and going in and out of this entrance. He wouldn't lack for targets.

As he neared the entrance, though, eight figures separated from the crowd and formed a half circle in front of him, about ten yards away.

"We're not going to let you do it, son. Lay down your weapons. You're under arrest."

Summers whipped the AR-15 up from where it was hidden under his coat, but he hesitated as he saw the clerical collar of Reverend Whitely. Then he noticed the way his left hand had his coat pulled back, the Glock holstered in front of his left hip. His head whipped around, took in all the clerical collars, all the Glocks.

"You may be able to kill a few of us, but there is no way you can kill us all. You will never enter this mall. It's over, son. Give it up."

Billy and I and the Reverend Moore were back on Billy's deck the next day. It wasn't quite 60 degrees in Huntsville today, and we had a Mason jar of Billy's special reserve against the chill.

"Looks like your TIME member in Minneapolis done just about perfect, Jim. Took that nut into custody without a shot fired."

We had all read the morning papers, which were full of the story about the eight ministers who had stared down a wanna-be mass killer

117

in front of the crowded mall. When interviewed about the incident, Reverend James Whitely had said it was their duty to protect people if they knew something was going to happen. But how did you know, was the question he was asked the most. "Ministers are very active in their communities. We see a lot of people every week. We have a good feel for what is going on. And people sometimes tell us things, tell us things in confidence, that are bothering them, or that they have heard. That's what our new organization does, it tries to put all these pieces of information together. And this time we got lucky."

"The young man obviously needs help, Billy. I hope that he gets it, now that the authorities are properly involved. And yes, Jim Whitely did a good job, recruiting others and training them up. He did a couple stints in the army between college and seminary, so he was already well-versed in the use of weapons, and he'd seen some tense situations himself."

I put in, "And it got us some publicity for your bunch, Jim, for TIME."

"Yes, indeed. I have already received emails from some ministers who had previously declined to become involved, so that's very positive. And I think the next time one of our members approaches the police, we will have a bit more credibility."

Billy picked up some printouts from the side table.

"Well, going to that point, Jim, we need to start workin' on the next one. This one here's a terrorist attack."

Autonomous

"Hey, Chief, we got a message here says that somebody's going to try to blow up the Super Bowl."

"Yeah. At the NFL briefing for law enforcement, they say they get crank bomb threats almost every year."

"This one's weird, though, Chief. It's very specific. Names names, addresses. About a dozen Islamic names here. Says they're going to disguise a van as a media van to get it inside the security perimeter, then drive it through the stadium main doors and blow it up during the game. Says it will bring down that whole section of the stadium, kill thousands."

"That'd be one hell of a bomb."

"No kidding. The other thing weird about this one, though, Chief, is the guy gives his name. Says he's a minister, Reverend Vernon Cranston, with some outfit called TIME."

"TIME? T-I-M-E, TIME?"

"Yeah, that's what it says."

"Holy.... Activate SWAT. And get the FBI on the phone right now."

"On a crank bomb threat?"

"That's no crank threat. Those are the same guys who headed off that Minneapolis mall shooting. And if they're right this time, it's gonna take a lot more than a half-dozen ministers with side arms to stop this."

"Well, Billy, looks like they're listening to the preacher and his buddies now." I waved the paper at Billy. It didn't say how the police and FBI knew about the bombers, but Billy and I both knew they had been warned by one of Reverend Moore's operatives.

"Yeah, that one was a big one, too. That whole side of the stadium was going to collapse, and kill a couple thousand people. So it's good we got 'em." Billy got up and waved me to follow him, and we headed for the pole barn. "Time for the follow-up run."

Billy had explained it to me. When we stopped one of these events, all of our existing data became worthless. We had changed the future, so now we had to get back in the truck and make another run. Maybe stopping the mall shooter kept another guy from doing something like that, because he didn't want to get caught, so one of our future shootings wouldn't happen. Wouldn't be good to set off a false alarm. We needed to keep a perfect batting average, or it could ruin TIME's reputation, make it hard to convince police to act. Or maybe the aborted mall shooting would inspire someone else, add a new incident that we would miss if we relied on old data.

I didn't look forward to it though. Time travel sounds exciting and all, but mostly it's just boring. After the mall shooting, Billy had rigged up cameras in the truck that were constantly rolling on all four screens, capturing the data. It limited how fast we could travel and still catch it all on the cameras. So we'd brought beer and sandwiches and cigars and a checkerboard, but mostly it was just a long boring sit in the truck. We got back out at the same time we left, but we were hours making that run.

"Yeah, but I'm not looking forward to it. You got the beer and sandwiches?"

"Nah, I got something better. You gotta see this."

Billy led me around to the driver's door, opened it, and gestured me to look inside.

"What did you do to the time lever, Billy?"

Mounted to the floor was some sort of mechanism with a servo rod connected to the time lever.

"Red, you are looking at an autonomous time machine."

"Autonomous?"

"Yeah, you know. Like those driverless cars. We set the timer here for how long we want it to go forward, then trigger it by radio control from outside the truck, and it does the run all by itself."

"Billy, that is genius, pure genius. I felt like a fifth wheel on that last trip. I mean, with the cameras rolling, we didn't do anything anyway but sit and drink."

"Yeah, now we don't have to just sit there while the time machine and cameras do their work. Not only that, we won't be there if something goes wrong."

"If something goes wrong? Whatcha talkin' about, Billy?"

"Red, this thing is a one-off, a lab piece. It's not, you know, off some assembly line or something. It's more like an experimental plane than an airliner. We been test pilots on this thing, but I don't have any idea how long it's gonna keep workin'. Even so, if it was 5 years or 50,000 miles, I figure we got about five years of running into the future clocked up on this thing already. Everything wears out sooner or later, and I'd just as soon not be in it when it does."

I just stood there looking at him, running through it in my mind.

"OK, but what if this thing does blow up? We're gonna be just standing here."

"Yeah, but what it'll probably do is just not run. If it does blow up, it oughta be in the future, so we'll make sure not to be around when it does. Anyway, let's turn the cameras on and get her going. I got the timer set for about a six months run forward, then back."

We set the cameras, and Billy turned on the machine with the switch on the dash. We closed the doors, and swung the side monitors back into position. We always left them in position -- that's what we were recording in the future, after all -- but we swung them out of the way to get in and out.

Then we both stood back, and Billy pushed the remote control. And nothing happened.

"I guess it didn't work, Billy."

"Wanna bet? It went and just came back to the same time. Look at the cameras."

Sure enough, the cameras were flashing the warning light that they were running out of space on the memory cards.

"OK, now that's cool. Billy, you're wasted at NASA. This is pure genius."

"You said that already. Come on, let's pull the memory cards and see what we got."

Failure

We'd been doing the runs into the future and bringing back the information that allowed Reverend Moore and his TIME organization to inform authorities before various criminal and terrorist events happened for a couple years when I stopped out at Billy's with a new idea. Billy had been retired from NASA for a while now, and I retired about the same time, so we got together any day of the week it suited us. Billy was sitting out on the porch and I joined him.

"Billy, you know we been running the truck ahead six month or so, and checking it out, looking for these events to stop. But I remember you told me this whole time machine thing could stop working any time."

"Yep. I'm surprised it lasted this long."

"Well, I was thinking, Instead of going after these things piecemeal, more or less one event at a time, what say we sent the truck a ways out, and went after a bunch at once."

"Well now, we talked about this, Red. Once we change the future, we need to go back and take another look. Same events might not happen."

"No, I know. But I was thinking in terms of these terrorist guys. We could get all the names we could, and have TIME turn them over to the FBI, and they can do one of those 'fifty simultaneous arrests in twelve states' kinda deals they like. Thing I'm concerned about is, once the machine stops working, we don't have any new data at all. We need to break the back of this terrorist thing."

"We're gonna need some mighty big memory cards."

"That's one reason I brought it up. They just brought out some big ones, sixteen times bigger than we been using. I picked up a set this morning."

"Well, what the heck. Let's give it a shot."

So we went out to the pole barn, and Billy took the charger off the stack of deep-cycle batteries in the bed of the truck. We put the new super capacity memory cards in the cameras and got them rolling. Then we stepped back and Billy pushed the button.

And the truck exploded. Or it imploded. Or something. The 6000 pounds of truck, time machine, batteries, cameras and all disappeared, replaced with about 500 pounds of slagged debris hanging in mid-air in various places where the truck had been. All the debris fell to the ground, and that was it. No sound. Just truck, then debris.

"Looks like it broke."

"Broke! Billy, it disintegrated!"

"Well, the time machine broke, the truck disintegrated. Better to have been here than there, though, from the looks of things."

I looked at the debris, saw the slagged remains of one of the cameras in the smoking pieces.

"Hey, Billy, it looks like one of the cameras survived, sorta." I started to step forward.

"Now don't go messing with that, Red. Some of that stuff might be radioactive."

I called in through the man door. "Hey, Billy, come on. Get outta there."

Billy came walking out through the man door. "How the hell did you get out here so fast? Man, you just disappeared."

"You said the magic word."

"Abracadabra?"

"No. Radioactive. How can that stuff be radioactive? What was that time machine made out of anyway?"

"Well, now, Red, when NASA builds a time machine, I think you can count on it that not all of the parts are something you can buy down 't the hardware store."

"No, I get that, but still...." I looked in through the man door toward the wreckage. "Billy, what are we gonna do now? Sometime in the future, that thing is gonna blow up."

Billy looked around the valley, at his house, and the guest house, then back at the pole barn. "Sure gonna make a mess. Probably first thing we oughta do is get a Geiger counter."

So we went into Huntsville to the science supply store and got a good Geiger counter. We started with readings from outside the pole barn, then moved inside, but everything was cold. We tested the Geiger counter again against the test sample we picked up and it worked fine. So we dug around in the debris and pulled out the one camera that had come back. It was so badly slagged that Billy had to clamp it down to the bed of the milling machine and machine his way in to the memory card.

"Think the memory card will still work?"

"Could be. It was protected pretty well by the camera. Only one way to find out."

We took the memory card into the house and put it in the computer. It had just over four and a half years of data on it. Billy copied it all to an empty hard drive big enough to hold it.

"OK, so we got a copy of it all now. I don't trust that card to last much longer after all that abuse, so it's good we got a copy off it before it failed. Now what, Red?"

"I think we need to go talk to Jim."

So we found ourselves once again in the office of the Reverend James Moore. We told him the story of the truck blowing up, probably rather impressively, four and a half years from now, and asked his advice.

"First, I think you need to make sure no one gets injured or killed. You fellows have the resources now to buy up that whole valley, so no one else lives there. But will the damage be limited to the valley?"

"I been thinking about that on the way over here, Jim. I think I can bunker up the pole barn to minimize the horizontal shock wave. Shoot it straight up instead."

"OK, so that's the second thing you need to do, build that bunker. I think you're right about the data. If we can put together all the terrorist information from the data you recovered, then we could turn that all over to the FBI at once, and they could investigate from there. The criminal events, the mass shootings, we can issue warnings about, not claim certainty because of the risk of using old data from the unaltered future, but we can still help.

"Which leaves us with the legal issues you boys are going to be facing. One thing I can offer there is that it often helps to have friends in high places."

"But we don't know anybody like that, Jim. We don't have any big-shot political friends."

"Think about it, Red. You have quite a bit of money, and you will have much more coming in, right?"

"Yeah, sure. When you know what's gonna happen in advance, the stock market is like shooting fish in a barrel. We can pretty much have however much money we want. But we still don't know any big shots."

"But you have four and a half years, and lots of money, and the big shots you need may not even be big shots now. For example, you know who the next president is going to be, right? And who the next attorney general is going to be, right?"

"Well, yeah, we can look that stuff up in the data, sure."

"And they aren't yet in such exalted office, right? So I only have one question for you.

"Have you ever written a check for a million dollars?"

Mitigation

Billy and I had our hands full. We were simultaneously trying to buy out all of Billy's neighbors so we owned the whole valley, design a containment system for the pole barn to contain, or, more precisely, direct the explosion, get to be real good friends, which is to say donors, with politicians we knew would be in positions of influence four and a half years from now, and make enough money in the stock market to finance it all.

Making the money turned out to be the easy part. My brother continued to run the trades we suggested, and the money piled up fast. Which was good. We would need quite a bit of spreadin' around money to ensure they didn't lock us up and throw away the key after the humongous explosion we knew was coming.

With Reverend Moore's help, we figured out which politicians would be the most useful to have as friends. The president and vice-president, sure. The attorney general, for whom the local district attorney worked. The DHS secretary, for whom the FBI worked. The chairman of the homeland security committee. The chairman of the appropriations committee.

Not the current ones, of course. The future ones. Who were often much less elevated now, more approachable, and more in need of funds.

So with Reverend Moore's help, Billy and I went into Huntsville, and we got fitted out with some spendy suits, shirts, ties, shoes, fancy watches -- the works. We both got real nice haircuts and beard trims while we were there. Fellow downtown on Jefferson Street by the courthouse does really nice work.

We began going to increasingly expensive fund-raising dinners around the South. At first we were sort of curiosities, the good ol' country boys hanging out with the big shots. But Billy and I could both tell a pretty good yarn or crack a witty remark, and pretty soon people were happy to see us, and even happier if they were seated at our table. Our new friends would often stop in to Huntsville and pick us up at the airport in their chartered planes.

It wasn't long before people were asking us for contributions to this PAC or another. One of them was a target of ours, as it was associated with a couple of our target politicians. I asked "if two was enough", and when they said that would be nice, I wrote a check on the spot for two million dollars and watched their eyes bug out a little. I think they were thinking two thousand. When Billy said "and this here's from me" and handed them an identical check, I thought they was gonna faint. That's when we started getting invited to private meetings with the candidates. We actually got to be pretty good friends with the man who would be vice president, and me and Billy and Maggie and Sue spent a week with him and his wife at their place on Cape Cod during a Congressional recess.

Back home, we slowly bought out Billy's neighbors. Some were getting older and wanted to move into town. Others were amenable for other reasons. There was one couple that raised their kids there, and were determined to stay, so we paid five times what the property was worth, telling them they could afford to put the grandkids through college with that kind of money. That sealed the deal.

Once we owned the whole valley, we closed off the road. County roads are really easements: the property owner owns to the center of the road. If you own both sides of a dead-end county road, you can close it off all the way back to the first property on either side that you don't own. So we put up a gate on the road and put up private property/no trespassing signs.

The only real trouble was getting the bunker built.

"Billy, you can't knock the pole barn down. The computers and all in there is what we were filming to get the data. They have to be there in the future."

"No they don't, Red. That all happened already. We already copied the data into the computer."

"Yeah, but that's because we filmed the monitors in the future. That hasn't happened yet. If you tear down the pole barn, the monitors won't be there to film."

"Red, we already copied the data. What's it going to do, disappear? The past happened, it's done, unchangeable. So, now we got the data, we don't need the monitors. We only needed them if we were going to keep going into the future."

"Billy, this time machine stuff drives me crazy."

The negotiations with the contractor were interesting, too. Billy had drawn up plans for a forty foot inside diameter concrete tube, with five foot thick walls, eighty feet tall.

"So, Mr. Green, what you want is to tear down the existing building, dig 20 feet down to bedrock, and then build this concrete structure in that exact spot?"

"Steel-reinforced concrete, with a tested strength of 25 MPa or better. And I want the rebar anchored into the bedrock with angle-drilled rebar on two foot centers, epoxied into the rock to a depth of at least three feet."

"Anchored into the bedrock?"

"Yep. I don't want it to move."

"Mr. Green, eight million pounds of concrete is unlikely to move."

"I just want to be sure. You wanna build it or not?"

The numbers were kind of crazy. It would take 210 truckloads of concrete, weigh over eight million pounds, and be a quarter of a million dollars just for the concrete, not including labor, forms, pumping the concrete sixty feet up into the air. But Billy wasn't done.

"And I want it girdled with half-inch steel cable under tension, every two inches."

"I assumed that was a misprint. Every two feet, right?"

"Every two inches, from top to bottom, all eighty feet of it."

"Mr. Green, that is over 15 miles of half-inch steel cable."

"You got a problem selling me steel cable? Think how much they used on the Brooklyn Bridge. This is nothing."

The problem was, we didn't really know how big the explosion was going to be. Billy hoped he had overbuilt, but we couldn't be sure. He also had the woods cut back to a 100-yard radius from the silo, because he didn't want the radiant energy of the plume out the top of the silo to start a forest fire.

So Billy and Maggie moved the double-wide and the single-wide over to some nice wooded property on the other side of town. And we told Reverend Moore to have TIME warn the authorities to have a ten-mile-radius no-fly zone for the first twelve hours of that day. He centered the no-fly zone a couple miles from the property, along the state highway, so the cops wouldn't be swarming around the property trying to figure out what was going on when the darned thing went off.

The day before the explosion, we collected up all the documentation about the time machine, all the computer hard drives, all the data we had about the whole thing, and destroyed it. We burned up all the written data, and we destroyed the hard drives and memory sticks with thermite, turning them into slag.

It was fall. At 6:30 in the morning, it was still dark, with just a hint of light in the eastern sky. Billy and I were in town, where the city park had a pretty good view to the south.

At 6:32, the missing 5500 pounds of Billy's truck fell out of the collapsing time bubble and turned into a rapidly expanding ball of superheated plasma. The plasma jet shot out of the top of the silo thousands of feet in the air, and was visible over fifty miles away. The plasma jet lasted less than a second. Thirty seconds later, a loud thunderclap rolled over the downtown.

At 8:00, when they opened for the day, Billy and I, accompanied by our high-priced D.C. lawyers, called on the FBI office in Huntsville.

The Attorney

Billy and I told the head of the Huntsville FBI office our story, from the time Billy mounted the ex-NASA time machine in his pickup truck until the truck fell out of the collapsing time bubble and vaporized inside Billy's concrete silo. At our direction, the FBI man had pulled in the director of the NASA Huntsville facility, the district attorney, and the local ATF guy before we started. The SEC had no representative in Huntsville, so we didn't have anyone from there. When we finished, the FBI man looked pretty angry.

"So you are turning yourself in?"

"No, my clients are not turning themselves in, Mr. Richards. They have broken no laws. This is an informational visit only, so you all know what happened, and you can pronounce your investigation closed."

"Broken no laws, Mr. Goldman? Broken no laws? I beg to differ. Operating a dangerous machine, that's reckless endangerment of the public, setting off an explosive device, securities fraud, theft of government materials, withholding information from law enforcement, bribery of government officials, and I'm just getting started." The district attorney and the ATF guy nodded, and, with that encouragement, the FBI man was getting ready to launch again when our attorney cut him off.

"My clients have broken no laws whatsoever, Mr. Richards. Let's take them one at a time, shall we? This "dangerous machine" you referred to is the time machine that NASA directed Mr. Green to discard. Is that correct?" The FBI man nodded and Mr. Goldman went on. "I submit to you that it was not known to be a dangerous machine. Consider. It is my understanding that NASA operated this very machine at their facility here in the Huntsville metropolitan area, approximately five miles from downtown Huntsville. The machine was operated with no special precautions, without any sort of bunker protection or other safeguards. Clearly, NASA did not consider it a dangerous machine, or, if they did, they are in serious trouble." The NASA guy blanched. "But my clients, having relied on NASA's assessment, are clearly not guilty of reckless endangerment. And, unlike NASA, they operated it in a rural area, not in the center of a highly populated metropolitan area.

"As to the charge of setting off an explosive device, I assume you are referring to a violation of 18USC Section 844. First, a time machine is not considered an explosive device or material under the code. Second, there was no intent to cause an explosion. The device, operated as it was intended to be operated, failed, and that failure caused an explosion. Explosions often occur when a device fails or due to some human error. Tragically people are often injured or killed in such explosions. I am reminded of houses that explode due to the failure of a gas furnace. Are the homeowners in such cases charged with setting off an explosion, Mr. Urbanski?" The ATF guy reluctantly shook his head no. "I see. Such a charge in this case is equally unwarranted, and may constitute malicious prosecution. Especially since, once they became aware that an explosion might occur, my clients spent several million dollars to purchase the affected area, to construct a deflection silo that limited its effects on people and property, and in fact no one was killed or injured and no property other than their own was damaged." That last was with a nod to the district attorney, who looked thoughtful. Mr. Goldman considered his notes.

"Let's see, securities fraud. It's too bad the SEC couldn't have a representative here. I trust you will later inform them of the conclusion of your investigation. With regard to that, though, there is no mention in the code of a time machine, and no provision that makes it illegal to act on any information so obtained. While my clients' investment technique is certainly unconventional, and by all accounts highly successful, it is not -- currently, at least -- against the law."

"But between them they made over 500 million dollars!"

"Indeed. As I said, highly successful, but not illegal. Your next item, I believe, was theft of government materials. Mr. Green, I understand, was directed by his superiors to scrap the machinery upon the cancellation of the project by NASA. Further, Mr. Green purchased the machinery from NASA as scrap. Mr. Green, do you have a receipt for that purchase?"

Billy reached into his coat pocket and pulled out a folded receipt written on NASA stationery and handed it to Mr. Goldman. I hadn't found out Billy had actually purchased the machine until we had been first interviewed by our attorneys a month ago.

"You should make a copy of this for your investigation file, Mr. Richards. It shows that my client purchased the machine and all relevant documentation for $350. Note that that was for 700 pounds of scrap metal, for which the going rate is more like a dollar per hundred pounds. It sounds to me like NASA did pretty well on the deal, Mr. Walz." The NASA guy winced.

"As to the charge of withholding information from law enforcement, the record shows my clients did the exact opposite. They sought out information of use to law enforcement, founded an organization to communicate this information to law enforcement, which, by the way, did not initially believe or act on that information, thereby placing thousands of people in a crowded shopping mall at risk and making it necessary for several members of the local clergy to intervene, at considerable risk to themselves. Mr. Richards, do you have any record as to the number of criminal and terrorist actions that were disrupted through the use of information provided to law enforcement by my clients through the TIME organization?"

"More than a hundred."

"One hundred and fourteen to be precise, Mr. Richards. And that does not include the actions that would likely have been committed by the 153 individuals with terrorist connections that the FBI simultaneously arrested in 27 states three years ago using information provided by my clients. I note also that my clients and their organization were never mentioned in FBI press releases as the source of the information that resulted in those arrests or disrupted these attacks, which would have killed thousands of Americans. The FBI instead gave credit to their own internal investigations. In any public trial, that will certainly come out. And if the news reporters fail to take sufficient notice, I think you can count on me to point it out to them." It was the FBI guy's turn to wince.

"We now come to the charge of bribery of government officials. A serious charge. My own research indicates that my clients have made sizable donations to political action committees supporting the election of several high ranking officials, including the president, the vice president, the attorney general, the chairman of the House Appropriations Committee, and the Secretary of Homeland Security, but have not asked for, received, or expect any quid pro quo, which is required to prove any case of bribery."

"But it makes them immune to prosecution!"

"Perhaps. That is not my decision to make, gentlemen, that is your decision. In that context, however, I think you need to consider this. To prosecute, on trumped-up charges in my view, which I will be more than happy to share with the media, two people who have saved the lives of thousands of Americans over the last seven years, on their own initiative and at their own expense, and for which federal agencies took all the credit, would not go over well with the public. Or the administration, I suspect."

The Agreement

Billy and I had told the FBI, NASA, and the district attorney all about our adventures with the time machine, and our attorney had pretty much made it clear to them that they were gonna have to let us off scot-free, or else. They asked for a break to confer with each other, and Mr. Goldman told them we would return after lunch. There was some consternation at the idea of us just walking out of there, at which point Mr. Goldman noted that we had come to them, after all, and we weren't in custody, now were we? They quickly said we weren't, and we went out for a very pleasant lunch, then were back in the FBI office with the same players as before. The NASA director spoke first.

"Mr. Goldman, we would like to hire your clients to build another time machine. As it turns out, all the documentation of what was done was sold to Mr. Green, as you noted, and according to Mr. Green was in the truck when it exploded. Further, the two senior scientists critical to its development retired a few years ago and have since

131

passed away. I am afraid that the only person remaining who has the knowledge to construct another such device is Mr. Green."

Mr. Goldman raised an eyebrow to Billy.

"Nope. Won't do it. I know you could use it for police work, saving lives and such, like we did, but would that be all? To have a bunch of bureaucrats and government types with a machine like that? Go ahead a bit, look at election results, come back and tell some politician to ignore this state, spend more money in these five counties of that state, change the results of an election, change who gets to be president. I just don't trust ya, and I ain't gonna do it. We gave money to politicians, but we only gave it to the guys we knew were gonna win already, and we done that just to protect ourselves from you folks. Met some nice people, too. The vice president, he's a helluva guy, and his wife's a sweetheart." Billy looked off into the distance and smiled at some memory of our times together with the vice president, then looked back at the NASA guy. "Nope. Won't do it, and that's that."

"But you have to!"

"No, Mr. Walz, he certainly does not have to. There is no legal authority that can force my clients to create another time machine. And, for what it's worth, I agree with Mr. Green's reasoning. The idea that the federal bureaucracy would have a device like that is more than a little terrifying."

They went off to confer among themselves for a bit while we had coffee and looked out the windows at the view of downtown Huntsville. When we got back together, they had a couple of non-disclosure agreements for us to sign. They basically wanted the whole thing hushed up. I couldn't blame them. Mr. Goldman reviewed the documents.

"The only problem I see here, gentlemen, is that this is essentially an employee non-disclosure agreement, but my clients are not now employees of the federal government, and even in Mr. Green's case have not been for years. Throughout most of the period of interest, in fact."

They looked back and forth for a minute before the FBI man spoke.

"Do you have any suggestions, Mr. Goldman?"

"Well, you could make them federal government employees. You know, back date the records to make them both NASA employees, say, Senior Scientists, throughout the period of interest. Not carried openly on the books until now, secret project, hush-hush, all that. Then they could sign these agreements, and the agreements would cover all of their activities throughout the period."

After some hurried discussion, they all agreed that that would work, but then Mr. Goldman threw them a curve ball.

"The only thing remaining then is the financial aspect."

"The financial aspect?" That was the FBI man.

"You are going to make them NASA employees throughout the period of interest. That amounts to some seven years of back pay."

"What?" That was the NASA guy.

"Of course. How are you going to claim they were employees if they weren't paid? The non-disclosure agreements would be unenforceable. And since this whole time machine project they were working on was for NASA, because after all these agreements specify non-disclosure with respect to work-related activities, there is also the matter of their expenses. The purchase of all the cameras and batteries and computers and monitors and internet services used in the time machine operations, the purchase of all the land in the valley, and the construction of the silo, to mitigate the effects of the time machine's failure, and the loss of Mr. Green's pickup truck."

There was a fair amount of outrage all around on that. Then Mr. Richards played his trump card.

"They would have to return all the money they made in the stock market then. That was part of this whole thing, too."

"No, I don't think so, Mr. Richards. Those investments were made on their own time, and with their own money. They did use information from the project to do it, but at the time, they were not covered by these non-disclosure agreements. I don't think you can make that stick." They hesitated, and then Mr. Goldman played his trump card. He pulled his cell phone out of the holster on his belt and set it on the conference table. "Or, we can walk out of here without signing these agreements, having no duty of non-disclosure at all. Instead, I can just turn this recording of my clients' story and our discussions over to the New York Times."

"You recorded this meeting?"

"And you didn't, Mr. Richards?" That at least got a blush out of the FBI man.

"You wouldn't dare turn that over to the papers."

"On the contrary, Mr. Richards. If it is required to protect my clients from the government, I am duty-bound as their attorney to do so."

So there was a lot of grumbling, especially when Mr. Goldman presented them with NASA expense reports already all filled out with all of Billy's and my expenses, which totaled up to several million dollars. NASA ended up owning the whole valley as a "remote testing site", including the big silo, which had actually held up pretty well, considering. Billy and I got back pay, which enhanced his retirement payments as well, and we got to keep all the money we made in the stock market. Mr. Goldman and the FBI man agreed to destroy their respective recordings of the meeting, and Billy and I signed the NASA non-disclosure agreements.

So that's the story of how Billy and I bought a time machine for three hundred fifty dollars, made over half a billion dollars in the stock market, saved thousands of lives, got hundreds of criminals and terrorists arrested, got to be good friends with the president, the vice president, and lots of other politicians and celebrities, made the DA, the FBI, NASA, the ATF and the SEC really, really mad at us, set off the biggest firecracker in the history of Alabama, and got away with it all.

Keep it under your hat, though, OK?

Sha'nel

Sha'nel had left her traveling party at their base camp at dawn, as she had been instructed. The climb since had been strenuous but not difficult, as she was still in the flower of youth, and well built.

The peak was marked with a cairn of stones. She stopped a hundred yards distant, and set down her pack. She removed her dusty traveling clothes, her cloak, her blouse, her skirts, her bindings, until she stood naked in the wind blowing across the peak. She removed from her pack the vial of oil and anointed herself, just a touch, at her forehead, her breast, her palms, and her feet. Shivering, she removed the ceremonial clothes from her pack and donned them, woolen trousers, blouse, heavy fleece tunic, vest of mail, boots, gloves, and helm.

She removed from her pack the pouch of kindling, and her flint and stone. The kindling was from the great tree that grew in the courtyard of the Keep of Kor'dal the Great. The Keep was the seat of government, where the Elders of the Thirty Villages met in the great throne room. Where, every three years, they elected one of their number as The Eldest, she to rule in the queen's stead. The Throne itself sat empty on its dais. Not for four hundred years had a queen ruled in Logarn. For four hundred years, there had been peace.

The wind whipped at her long black hair as she looked out across the world. Gamrok was the highest peak of the range, on the clearest days visible even from the capital itself, the holy mountain that appeared on Logarn's flag beneath dragon rampant. Away north and south its lesser brethren stretched to the horizon, while to the east spread the fields, farms, and villages of Logarn. To the west, hills marched down to the sea.

Taking up the vial of oil, Sha'nel approached the cairn. To the east of the cairn, she knelt and dug a small depression in the loose gravel, and filled it with kindling from the pouch. She made a pocket in the side of the little pile, into which she placed the finest shavings. She huddled over the depression, shielding it from the wind, as she used flint and stone to spark the shavings, then blew them alight. As the fire grew, she added more of the kindling, until the entire pouch was emptied upon the fire.

She folded her legs under her, and sat facing the cairn over the fire. She emptied the small vial of oil over the fire, and the fire flared up. She then picked up a sharp stone from the gravel about her, and dug the point into the fleshy heel of her hand. Forcing a single drop of blood from the puncture, she dripped it on the fire, laid her hands open upon her knees, and waited.

Sha'nel had no idea what she was waiting for. Her single task was to travel to the mountain, scale its peak, make this offering at the cairn, and wait. The same offering was made in the courtyard of the Keep every week by herself or one of the other twenty-nine acolytes that attended the Elders. When she had asked the Eldest what she was to wait for, she had only smiled and said, "You will see." "But how will I know if my offering is worthy?" "You will know."

And so she waited. She thought about this task, a hopeless last offering to the uncaring gods on the eve of war. For four hundred years, no one had dared attack Logarn. The legend said Logarn was invincible, despite having no army. But a warlord had swept up Logarn's smaller neighbors in conquest. He had built a great army that was even now preparing to attack Logarn.

There was a sound of rock sliding on rock. Sha'nel stared transfixed as the stones of the cairn shifted and flowed into each other. The cairn became the bent seated figure of a naked, wizened old man. The bowed head lifted, and piercing green faceted eyes glittered in the firelight as they peered at Sha'nel.

"Who summons Gamrok?" his deep voice rumbled.

"I am Sha'nel, an acolyte of Logarn."

"I may not be summoned save in the direst cause. Show me."

The old man's eyes grew in Sha'nel's vision until she was lost in them. She felt another mind, an ancient and cunning mind, enter her memories, memories of the long peace of Logarn, defenseless but for the thirty acolytes, and the army now on its borders. The alien mind withdrew.

"All is as it should be. You and your people have kept faith with the agreement I made with your ancestor, Sha'nel of Logarn. And so Gamrok and his people will keep faith with you."

"Agreement?"

"A thousand years and more ago, Kor'dal and I became unlikely friends. My people had wandered the nations of men, seeking a home. But the turmoil of war, the screams of women and children, these allow no peace for such as we. Kor'dal invited us to live here, in these mountains, unmolested, and agreed to make no war, to keep no standing armies, to forsake conquest for a life of peace for all of Logarn. In return, we guaranteed the safety and peace of Logarn."

"You? You guarantee the peace of Logarn?"

His deep chuckle seemed to shake the very ground. "Do not be fooled by appearances, young one. I and my people were born from the very bones of the earth in the beginnings of time. My shape is of my choosing."

The old man bowed his head, and flowed down into the rock once more. Sha'nel jumped back as the cairn began to grow, pushing up out of the ground, getting larger as it pushed upward. Higher and higher it rose, the rock flowing as it uncoiled. Towering over her head, the rock took the form of a great dragon, three hundred feet long, more, a gigantic beast out of myth and legend. Six great feet clutched the ground with six-foot talons, a spiny crest ran down its back from head to tail, and it was covered in armored plates the size of a man's shield. It spread enormous wings, lifted its head, and with a great gout of flame let out a roar that echoed across the mountains.

The sinuous neck stretched out and down to Sha'nel until the great head was directly in front of her, one vast green-faceted eye looking directly into hers. "Mount your steed, Sha'nel, Queen of Logarn."

"Queen?"

"Only one of the blood of Kor'dal can summon forth Gamrok the Great. Only the Queen may ride me to war. You were chosen. It is your destiny. Ride now, to the defense of your people."

Sha'nel mounted the neck of the giant beast, taking a seat behind the great head between two of the spines running down its neck, and Gamrok lifted from the mountaintop. Around them, twenty-nine other dragons, summoned by Gamrok's war cry, rose from the neighboring peaks and followed them into the east.

RICHARD F. WEYAND

The Lahan Wars I
Hero of the Captaincy

The battle had not gone well.

Fleet Commander Pitjara held the three-dimensional display in his mind as the command ship's computer updated it with a continuous feed of sensor data. Few enough ships now, he noted, after their horrendous losses. Barely two hundred ships accelerated madly away from the pursuing enemy, leaving the drifting wreckage of hundreds of ships behind. The remaining operational enemy ships, over three hundred of them, raced in pursuit. And they were gaining.

I hate this damned war.

The current hostilities had lasted his entire military career, and that was just the latest phase of a war that had raged off and on for generations. The various planetary governments had fought to exhaustion, to the limits of their economies, their populations, and their resources. Spent, they planned, re-armed, formed new alliances and confederations among themselves, seeking advantage, then staggered back into space and fought again. Again and again the cycle repeated, and never a resolution.

He turned his attention to the prize. Lahan, the mother planet of myth and legend, rent by a volcanic cataclysm millennia ago. Thousands of cubic kilometers of ash, millions of tons of sulfates and thousands upon thousands of cubic miles of steam all propelled into the atmosphere had pushed the planet into a deep and sudden ice age. Most of those that did not die in the initial cataclysm and its immediate aftermath had starved to death or died in the fall into savagery. Hundreds of millions had died, a mere few thousand had survived.

The colonies, dependent on the technology and resources of the mother planet, had been forced to fall back on their own meager resources. Much of their technology was lost in that fight for survival. It had taken thousands of years for them to recover, to regain space. When they had, they found Lahan reborn, green and rich and fertile.

Each would have it, none would concede. And so they fought, and died, and fought again.

He looked at that blue and green orb in his mental display -- the ultimate prize, which could not be had but could not be left to another -- and he hated it. Lahan, graveyard of navies. Here was the reason they fought and died. Whichever colony possessed its riches -- its water, its minerals, its plant and animal life, and its environment, in which the people had arisen and to which they were most well-adapted -- must eventually rule all of explored space. None could leave it alone or concede it to another. It would be better to leave it to its miserable savages, descendants of that long-ago cataclysm, than to fight and die for millennia to no end. But none could do so unless all did.

He turned his attention back to the remnants of his fleet and its eager pursuers. For three days they had been fleeing the enemy, playing out the end game of the short and violent battle. *It won't be much longer. Perhaps one more day. Perhaps less.*

Fleet actions were seldom decisive. Space was too big and the targets too small. More common was a battle of attrition, with opposing fleets wearing each other down until one was forced to withdraw. The small, fragile ships shot ballistic projectiles, long metal rods, with their axial electromagnetic impellers. An impact on one of the fragile ships almost certainly resulted in the destruction of the ship and the loss of all aboard, but the tiny ships were very hard to hit, defended by their own insignificance in the vastness of space.

The small size of the ships was the result of generations of experience. Large ships were too easy to hit, too slow on the helm and too structurally fragile. Such a large amount of materials and personnel in one location was easily defeated by a numerous and faster force of small ships using the same amount of materials and people. The optimum size had settled around a thousand metric tons with a crew of about forty. Any smaller and they could not accommodate the gravitation displacement drive, even in its smallest form.

The projectile technology had advanced over the years. Faster projectile velocities gave less time for evasive maneuvers. Faster cycle times put more projectiles in space toward the target. Multiple small rods in a plastic casing that disintegrated on acceleration generated a spread of projectiles and a greater probability of impact. Small jets at one end of each rod started them tumbling, increasing their impact cross-section. All of these had improved miniscule hit percentages, but battles were still long, drawn-out affairs that were generally inconclusive.

Which did not mean that people didn't die, but it was seldom so one-sided a battle as this one had been.

He had maneuvered his fleet for days to force the enemy into action on his terms, and he had succeeded. *Too well, in fact.* The enemy had a new wrinkle in their weapons system, and it had proved devastating. They were firing two-piece hollow rods, filled with a thousand meters of carbon monofilament. When fired, the two pieces would spring apart, paying out the monofilament between them. The resulting impact cross-section was huge, with a corresponding increase in the hit percentage. When the monofilament did contact a ship, even if it didn't cut into the ship itself, it would draw one or the other of the halves across the hull, ripping a huge rent as it went.

He had sought this engagement, sought to press home his numerical advantage, and he had been mousetrapped. The enemy's hit percentage was still small, but it was much higher than his own, and the importance of that difference was spelled out in the fields of drifting wreckage they had left behind as they tried desperately to escape.

His crews were in shock, he knew. Young and brash and full of their own immortality, they could not even conceive of such a loss. His own reputation just made it worse. Hero of the Captaincy of Gubam, his home planet, honored for his defeat -- not decisive; nothing in this damned war was decisive! -- of the enemy fleet almost seven years before. He had been decorated before cheering crowds by the Captain himself, the ruling autarch of Gubam, direct descendant of the original Captain of the first colony ship to reach the planet. How could he have led them into such a terrible defeat? How could their superior fleet have been so outmatched?

Hero of the Captaincy, yet now they raced for their lives. *A race we are losing.*

The gravitation displacement drive created a gravitational field that was away from the ship on both ends, toward two poles. Move the ship off equilibrium toward the forward pole, and the ship accelerated, falling into a hole of its own making. Move the ship off equilibrium toward the aft pole, and the ship decelerated, falling into a hole behind it that it also carried with it. There always had to be two poles, for if you bent space-time on one side of the ship, you had to bend it back on the other.

The engines themselves were in the center of the ship, and the perceived gravity there was always zero because the ship on average was always in free fall. Under acceleration, sheer forces made "down" forward in the front half of the ship, as the field strengthened toward the pole. Similarly, perceived "down" in the back of the ship was aft, as the ship was falling faster than the gravitational field strength so far from the pole. Particularly disorienting for new recruits was that the direction of perceived gravity aboard ship was the same whether the ship was accelerating or decelerating. Everything always fell toward the ends of the ship.

He overlay the gravitational distortions of the various ships' drives onto his mental plot. He could see the poles of each of his ships as well as those of the enemy ships, which illustrated another problem. The enemy's poles were slightly further apart, and their ships slightly further off equilibrium, than his own. A small difference, but a telling one. The enemy was out-accelerating his fleet, pressing a minor advantage in the field strength of their drives. They had gradually made up the velocity difference he had gained with his initial maneuvers to bring them to action, and were slowly closing the distance again. It would not be long before they were within range to finish off his survivors.

He had initially thought that his ships were faster, and his initial maneuvers had pressed that advantage. In fact, the enemy's new ships could accelerate faster than his, but they were much slower to spool up. He had caught them with their poles at less than full strength, conserving energy, or perhaps just sucking him in for the kill. It did take huge amounts of energy to generate the poles, and it also took energy and skill to maintain ship separations because the poles themselves were gravitationally attractive. Running such large poles continuously at full strength could make ship handling within a fleet difficult.

His rambling thoughts skidded to a halt. *I wonder....*

Stowing the poles was as hard or harder than generating them. When a ship stowed the poles, the prodigious energy that had been put into distorting space-time to generate them came back and had to be stored in the superconducting toroidal coils that belted the center of the ship around the engines. That was the tricky part. When space-time sprang back, all that energy had to go somewhere, and the ship by definition occupied the center of the distortion. The coils could only be recharged safely so fast, and stowage time was roughly proportional to the spool-up time, and if that was so....

Fleet Commander Pitjara kept his voice and demeanor calm, almost disinterested, as he gave new orders. *Always the command face, even when you were in trouble. Especially when you were in trouble.* "Fleet course change, Wing Commander. Come to heading 110 degrees, same plane. Maintain fleet flank speed."

"Aye, Fleet Commander. Heading 110 degrees, same plane. Maintain fleet flank speed." His fleet navigation officer considered his own mental display for a moment. "But, Sir, that course will take us directly into --" He cut himself off as the Fleet Commander turned his head to raise a single eyebrow in his direction. "Yes, Sir. 110 degrees, same plane. Executing now, Sir."

Fleet Commander Pitjara watched as the fleet angled to the left in his mental display, closer to the gas giant they were approaching. He had headed here instinctively, hoping to buy time dodging among its moons or leveraging its gravitational field. With a gravitation displacement drive, large gravitational fields were rough sailing, but they also gave advantages, particularly for the adept. His new course projected deep into the gravity well of the huge planet, well beyond safety margins. Wing Commander Kanalu had been right to criticize the move, but he passed the fleet order confidently. Fleet Commander Pitjara could almost hear his thoughts. The Fleet Commander was a Hero of the Captaincy after all, he had a trick up his sleeve, would wrest victory out of this debacle, would save us all!

If only it were so, Wing Commander. Such a slim thread to hang such heavy hopes upon!

He watched the enemy fleet change course as well, and could almost feel their fleet commander's glee at his course change. They would be able to cut the angle on him, come in inside of him, close the distance even faster.

Let's just hope you haven't thought through all the implications of your fancy new drives yet, Fleet Commander.

The two fleets continued to build speed on their new vector, speeding toward the looming giant, a baleful eye watching their approach.

"We're getting significant side loads now, Sir."

"Maintain course, Wing Commander."

"Aye, Sir."

The gas giant's gravitational field was pulling at his drives now, trying to merge their space-time distortions with its own. It had the effect of a huge cross-current in the gravitational sea they sailed, and it was trying to suck his ships into its vortex. He continued to run calculations on both his fleet and the enemy's as they angled deeper into the gravity well on their tangential approach. His ships were turned directly away from the planet now, trying to maintain course. Ultimately they began sliding toward the planet, despite full thrust applied against the gravitational tide.

"Sir!"

"Not yet, Wing Commander."

Just a bit further, just a bit closer to the capture radius for our velocity....

"Fleet Emergency Stow, Wing Commander."

"Aye, Sir! Fleet Emergency Stow!"

He watched the maneuver in his mental display as he felt himself go weightless. All of his ships recentered on their equilibrium points and lurched toward the planet as their acceleration against it dropped to zero. They began stowing their poles as fast as their coils could recharge. Faster in two cases, he noted, as two of his ships vaporized to plasma. *Another eighty dead on my hands.* As the ships' poles wound down, the planet's pull on them reverted to its normal gravity and the ships fell through a low parabola around it.

The enemy fleet repeated his maneuver too late. As they recentered, their larger poles were sucked harder into the gas giant's gravity well, and their slower stowage times sealed their fate. He watched as the entire enemy fleet slid past the point of no escape, the capture radius for their velocity, where the planet's pull on the ships in freefall would spiral them in rather than slingshot them around. They were doomed. *Another 12,000 dead. And this is victory.*

As his fleet swung around the giant planet and its velocity began carrying it clear, Wing Commander Kanalu turned to him.

"Brilliant, Sir, absolutely brilliant! A stunning victory!" In the cramped command cubicle, Wing Commander Kanalu turned to him with awed respect in his eyes and gave him the salute reserved for a Hero of the Captaincy.

I hate this damned war.

The Lahan Wars II
Penalty Clause

The Guild pilot ship, surrounded by a swarm of several hundred warships, appeared without warning. The ionization effects of their transit played back and forth among the ships like St. Elmo's fire for a few seconds, before the warships began to deploy into their attack formation. The pilot ship slowly fell behind, out of the scope of the impending action, as the warships engaged their drives and accelerated.

"Rough transit?" Mulga asked his visitor.

"Oh, the usual, I guess. I'm just getting a little old for this sort of thing." Konol sighed and relaxed back into the chair.

The two Guild pilots sat on the veranda of Mulga's mountaintop retreat, looking down the Ngoroman River Valley toward the plains 50 miles distant. The valley cut deep into the mountains, hewn by a river spawned by summer melt from the glaciers in the still higher mountains behind them. Torrents cascaded over sheer drops, the spray creating rainbows in the summer sun. The short-lived and fragile tundra flowers of summer were a sprinkle of color on the bare slopes this high above the treeline.

Or rather their avatars sat on the virtual veranda of Mulga's mountaintop construct. It was a very nice piece of virtualization; all the comforts of home combined with those stupendous views. The pilots themselves, of course, were still on their respective pilot ships. Each had piloted one of the warring fleets here, and both would be disinterested spectators of the battle to come. Either way the battle came out, the Guild had been paid for their transits.

"Well, at least you don't have to deal with His Obvious Superiority, General Courain," Mulga noted. "This fellow is unbearable. I have seldom seen such an ego, and one with so little justification, in my career."

"You will, you will. I've certainly seen my share. Now, with my seniority, I can refuse those assignments, though the Guild dispatcher doesn't like it. I have enough career points, though, that I won't be doing this much longer. A couple more transits, and I'm done."

"But won't you miss it? I can't imagine not spacing. It's all I ever wanted to do."

"And I felt the same way at your age. But once you've done it all -- and then some -- you start thinking about sitting on a real veranda drinking some real brandy."

"I suppose." Reminded, Mulga took a sip of his brandy and stared sightlessly down the valley. "What do you think is going to happen in the upcoming battle? Have you given it any thought?"

"Not really. From what I've seen of it, Admiral Yarran's battle plan is sound. I think his basic strategy was to catch General Courain off guard here in his mustering area, rather than wait to fight him at Lahan."

"At that, he's probably succeeded. There's been a lot of bluster, but little or no defensive preparation. The only reason General Courain is in this empty system is to organize his Wolok forces for an attack on Admiral Yarran's Makko forces at Lahan. He hasn't even started practicing fleet maneuvers yet."

"That's what Admiral Yarran's intelligence said. His thought was to catch General Courain unprepared, getting himself organized and not yet ready for an engagement. In any case, it should be interesting."

"Well, we've got some time. It will be real-time hours before anything really happens. How about a game of Jigalan?"

"I thought you'd never ask."

Hooked into their shipboard navigation computers at a 30:1 timescale, Mulga and Konol had subjective days to catch up with each other's news, play Jigalan, and kibitz the fleet maneuvers during the hours in which the warships deployed for battle.

"Well, he caught 'em flat-footed all right," Konol remarked as they watched the maneuvers unfold in another corner of their minds.

"Yup. Be interesting to see what General Courain will do to try to get out of this one. He's not known for giving up a position easily."

"I don't see how he can avoid it, unless he's willing to lose the bulk of his forces to hold this system, which isn't their real objective anyway. Better to fall back and live to fight another day. Wait until those reinforcements show up, then come back in at Admiral Yarran."

"Perhaps. But I'm not sure that he's mentally capable of such a decision. I just don't see any other way out, though."

Admiral Yarran pressed his advantage as General Courain tried to collect his forces to counter Admiral Yarran's moves, but it seemed General Courain would be late in getting them together. Being separated would allow his forces to be defeated in detail by Admiral Yarran's concentrated fleet.

Even if General Courain could get them together in the same volume of space, getting them on the same heading at the same velocity was another matter altogether, and that meant that they would only be concentrated for a short period of time before their respective velocities divided his forces again. Admiral Yarran need only time his arrival either before or after General Courain's forces were concentrated in order to catch them separated.

The warships themselves were small, little more than a thousand metric tons with a crew of forty. Experience had taught that larger ships just made bigger targets, and a single lucky shot could take one out, especially if the superconducting toroidal inductor that circled the waist of any gravitational displacement ship was hit. Smaller ships were also easier to make rigid enough to withstand high drive forces, and so were faster on the helm.

The smaller ships had a lot of firepower for their tonnage. Each had a single axial impeller for firing ballistic projectiles, long slender rods accelerated by electromagnetic induction, but a fleet of three hundred ships could put a lot of projectiles into space, and each impeller could be independently targeted.

Smaller than a thousand tons was impossible, as the gravitational displacement drive simply wouldn't fit into a smaller vessel, not while leaving any mass allowance for crew and weapons. Even so, that was smaller than the mass required for the interstellar drive of the pilot ships. At twenty thousand tons, they dwarfed the warships, and they carried no weapons and no crew save the pilot himself. It was a single-purpose vessel, and its entire mass was the interstellar drive. It did not even have an in-system drive: it had to be towed into berth by a grav-disp ship.

As space warfare had developed, the big ships of old had been essentially broken up into pieces, with the gun platforms, each with its own small in-system drive, operating separately from the large interstellar drive that moved them between systems. There was an additional benefit of this division. The capabilities required to become a pilot were vanishingly rare in the population, and there were never enough of them. The tremendous demand chasing the short supply gave the pilots' Guild the power to demand high fees, and their separate pilot ships allowed them to remain non-combatants in the battles fought between the fleets they piloted.

Thus was humanity's small and precious pool of interstellar pilots preserved.

"Well, now that's an interesting maneuver," Mulga noted. He and Konol were once again on the balcony, once again watching as the fleet maneuvers unfolded.

"Indeed. It looks as though, rather than engage Admiral Yarran, General Courain is planning to abandon the system. Their ship velocities look like they're trying to form up on your vessel for transit."

"I wouldn't have thought General Courain knew what retreat meant, but it sure looks like -- Huh. Well, I just received word to stand by for transit of General Courain's fleet, so he is going to abandon the system after all. Makes sense, though. They're only here to muster; there's nothing in this system worth fighting for."

"Looks like it will be a while before they're gathered. The ships are all at different velocities, coming in at different angles. And what are these two fellows doing over here?" Konol pointed out a pair of General Courain's warships that were not headed for Mulga's pilot ship, but were instead vectoring toward Konol's pilot ship.

"Looks like a couple of lost sheep decided to form up around the wrong shepherd. They'll figure it out soon and head back around. Rather sheepishly, I would say."

"Ouch. Well, we certainly have time for a bit more Jigalan before they get themselves sorted out. Let's go."

As General Courain's forces began clustering around the Guild ship, Admiral Yarran's formation broke up into hunting parties going after the stragglers. None of Admiral Yarran's ships fired toward those of General Courain's ships which had taken up formation around the Guild ship. There was always the possibility of a stray shot hitting the Guild ship.

The Guild had many possible ways of making its displeasure known over the loss of a Guild ship. They ranged from the unpleasant to the unthinkable, and no one wanted to find out just how upset the Guild would be and what its response would entail.

The Guild ships were unarmed and unassailable. The space about them was safe haven. That is how it had always been and always would be.

"What are these guys up to?" Konol asked.

The two stray Wolok ships had continued on course towards the safe haven of Konol's Guild ship while the rest of their forces tried to get to safe haven around Mulga's Guild ship. Admiral Yarran's hunting parties continued to wreak havoc upon General Courain's stragglers. One of those hunting parties was angling around toward the two strays, but did not yet have a shot that was acceptably clear of the Guild ship.

"Surrender, I suppose. It's not unknown, and they were caught on the wrong side of Admiral Yarran's forces from my ship."

"Could be, I guess. Most of these crews would much rather die quickly in space than be subjected to the typical surrender terms. Indentured labor on the capturing world is much like any other death sentence, but it takes a long time to execute."

"Touche. I have asked General Courain's staff about them, and they maintain all ships are trying to form up. They acknowledge that all ships will not make it, some having been destroyed by Admiral Yarran's forces, and others are still in evasive maneuvers. Maybe they're going to angle through your safe harbor while building velocity to pass through the hunting parties, try to increase their chances that way."

"Could be, I suppose, though it doesn't look like a good angle for them."

At that point, the two "strays" fired on the Guild ship.

Guild ships did not travel through space, they traveled around it. Mass bends space-time, creating gravitation. But when an n-dimensional volume is deformed, orthogonals to that volume in other dimensions are no longer parallel. The Guild ships translated vertically in this fifth dimension, in the direction in which the orthogonals were converging. They built velocity across the orthogonals through the use of a gravitational sail, or rudder, that deflected the ship horizontally as it moved vertically. Changing the angle on the sail when the ship moved back down the orthogonals towards the real-time plane provided additional displacement.

The process took massive amounts of energy, stored in a superconducting toroid around the Guild ships waist. This was similar to but much larger than the superconducting toroids of the grav-disp ships. The critical issue for Konol was that the conversion of the stored energy into the fields required to translate a Guild ship required time.

Time that he did not have.

"I have transmitted to your ship all of my records, including my personal records, for transport to the Guild and to my family," Konol said.

"I will personally ensure that they are conveyed to the proper recipients," Mulga replied. "But what am I to do with regard to General Courain? I think it's pretty obvious that these two ships were acting under orders to fire on your ship. General Courain's intent is to abandon Admiral Yarran's force here without Guild transport and move against Lahan in Admiral Yarran's absence. His orders to me to stand by for transport to Lahan make that clear."

"The Guild contract is clear. Guild ships are non-combatants, and the safety of all Guild ships is guaranteed by the contractee in paragraph seven. By firing on my ship, General Courain has breached the contract, and the penalty clause of paragraph seven is invoked. Please assure me that you will fully apply the penalty clause in response to my murder."

Mulga blanched. "But the penalty clause of paragraph seven has never been invoked. Ever. And I am a very junior partner in the Guild. Will the Guild back me up?"

"Do not forget that I am a senior partner in the Guild, and I sit on the Guild's contracts board. I have included in my final report my finding that General Courain has breached paragraph seven. You are therefore not acting alone, but under the authority of the contracts board. The Guild has therefore already decided the issue."

"In which case, I will be pleased to carry out the penalty. The Guild must act to protect its ships, or we will be potential targets in every battle, and humanity will lose its ability for interstellar travel."

"With all our business taken care of, what I would like most to do in the minutes I have left is to have one more go at you in Jigalan. You didn't think I would let that last victory of yours go unanswered, did you?"

The three minutes that it took the projectiles to traverse the distance to Konol's helpless pilot ship gave the Guild pilots ninety subjective minutes to do their final business and get in a couple last rounds of Jigalan. When the time drew to a close, Konol turned to the younger pilot.

"Fare well, my friend. Long life and safe transit."

And with that his avatar disappeared as, tens of thousands of miles away, his ship exploded.

General Courain's remaining ships, the bulk of his fleet, had taken up position for transport in the safe harbor area around the remaining Guild pilot ship. Admiral Yarran's ships watched helplessly as their erstwhile quarry prepared to run and leave his force stranded.

"But you cannot abandon us here while transporting the Wolok forces to Lahan," Admiral Yarran argued. "You are rewarding them for firing on a Guild ship."

"You are advised to wait here for transport, Admiral Yarran. The matter of the destruction of the Guild pilot ship is a contractual matter between Wolok and the Guild and does not concern you. Your transport is also a contractual matter, and the Guild will live up to its contract with Makko," Mulga replied.

"That will do me little good if General Courain is already in possession of Lahan by the time I get there."

Mulga floated in the five-space viewer, the universe spread out around him. It was the ability to use the viewer that was rare in humanity. Most people could conceptualize the concept of multiple dimensions in a crude way, but they could not experience them through the viewer.

Of course, the viewer only displayed four dimensions: x, y, z, and g. By convention, however, time was the fourth dimension, and the gravity dimension was five, so it was called a five-space viewer.

The computers that prepared the viewer display had no problem with the concept at all: any dimension was a mathematical construct to the computer, and four was as easy as three. Humans, though, had personal experience of three dimensions, and the person who could immerse himself in the viewer and see all four dimensions was very rare.

As the power continued to spool up, Mulga deployed his field about the Wolok ships and prepared for transit. When the power levels had stabilized, he released anchor from space-time, and began to rise in the gravitation dimension. He set his sails, and trimmed them to make way to his destination.

His destination was not Lahan.

The Guild pilot ship and its consorts appeared once again in the space-time plane. There was no star nearby, no planet. Nothing relieved the emptiness but the light of distant stars, the closest of which was ten light-years distant.

"This isn't Lahan! I order you to take us to Lahan immediately!" General Courain screamed over the comm channel.

Mulga appeared on the comm channel, or his avatar did, in full Guild dress uniform and ceremonial mask. The overall effect was meant to be intimidating, and emphasized his Guild membership over his individuality. "Wolok has been found by the Guild's contracts board to be in violation of paragraph seven of the Guild contract, for willfully firing upon and destroying a Guild pilot ship. By this act, Wolok has declared war upon the Guild. You and your ships are thus an enemy force, to be destroyed by the Guild as it may deem fit within the rules of war. Goodbye."

And with that, the Guild pilot ship, which had never wound down its fields, withdrew its field envelopment of the Wolok warships and disappeared back into grav-space.

The Guild pilot ship reappeared in the space-time plane approximately where Konol's ship had been destroyed.

"Admiral Yarran, I am here to fulfill the Guild's contract with Makko and to transport your ships to such destination as you see fit at this time," Mulga said.

"But where are General Courain's ships? What am I to find when I reach Lahan? Has he already taken the system?"

"I regret that I could not inform you earlier of the Guild's decision with respect to Wolok's destruction of the Guild pilot ship that transported you here. General Courain's ships were not transported to Lahan. By firing on a Guild pilot ship, Wolok declared war on the Guild. General Courain's ships were therefore transported into an area of empty space and left there. Further, no Wolok ship will be provided transport by the Guild, and no transport into or out of the Wolok system will be provided by the Guild, for a period of sixty years," Mulga said.

"Congratulations, Admiral," Mulga continued. "It seems you have won your battle, and your war, by default."

The Lahan Wars III
The Justice Algorithm

Honor Retained

"They want *what*?"

"A justice algorithm."

"What's a justice algorithm? Do we have a software specification for it?"

Pindan sighed and tipped back in his chair. "I don't know, and no, in that order. But that's what they want, and it's our job to come up with it."

"Oh, yeah? Who says?" Maki was the *enfant terrible* type of programmer: absolutely brilliant and just as hard to manage. But he was the best programmer in Pindan's group, and Pindan had the best staff of programmers on Gubam.

"The Captain of Gubam, the Autarch of Gumuny, the President of Wirra, the Emperor of Gorlondin, the King of Wolok, the Director of Makko, and over a dozen other planetary rulers and signatories to the Treaty of Ngurrun. You going to argue with them all? I'm not."

"Oh." Maki deflated for a moment, then gathered steam again. "But what is it? What's it supposed to do? We can't do anything unless they tell us what they want it to do."

"They want a computer program that will reach through the mental interface and inspect the memories of each citizen of Wurrpbu and Kornu, one at a time, analyze their memories for complicity in the illegal settlement of Lahan in violation of the Treaty of Ngurrun, and pass judgment on them."

Maki was speechless. For long seconds, he was absolutely struck mute. Pindan stared in fascination: he hadn't believed anything could quiet the voluble programmer for so long. Finally, Maki spluttered a response. "But, but that's -- I don't know what it is. It's monstrous. It runs counter to all the mental privacy regulations, even as weak as they are."

"I know. And it gets worse. The penalty for complicity with the violation of the treaty is death. They want the justice algorithm to execute sentence immediately, simply shut down the mental processes of the accused while in mental interface."

"Well, I know what I would do. I'd refuse the interface. Done." Maki folded his arms and nodded his head sharply. "No interface, no judgment, and no sentence."

"In which case, the administrators of the trials are to execute the accused immediately, by more, er, mechanical means."

"That's crazy! What about real trials, with real judges? Trial by computer algorithm? *Why?*"

"Because there are over a billion people altogether on Wurrpbu and Kornu, and they want to try them all. No exceptions. No villains to get away. You know your history. Do you want to go back to the Lahan Wars? You and I would have been on the fleets, shut up in those miserable little warships, fighting across space, to guarantee that no other planet gained possession of Lahan. We would probably be dead by now. Well, the rulers of all the Alliance planets know their history, too, so the alternative to trials is to simply kill them all, all the people on Wurrpbu and Kornu. Depopulate the planets entirely. Some of the Alliance rulers would rather do that anyway, but the Captain and a couple of the other rulers argued for this instead. So if we can automate the trials, make having a billion trials possible, and base the judgments on people's actual memories, then we can save all those people."

"And we *have* to do this?"

"They think we're the best group for the job. Think of it this way. Would you rather have someone *else* write this algorithm? Someone a little less fastidious about their programming, perhaps? Like Nowra and his group, for example? Or maybe Kulan and his group?" Pindan suppressed an involuntary shudder.

Maki sunk in his chair, his argument defeated. "No. No, I wouldn't. Someone might use it someday on me. The least we can do is be sure that it's the best it can be, I guess. I still don't like it."

"You and me both. But we have no choice, really. You and I are a long way from independent status, and as programmers indentured to the Captaincy, our options are very limited. Refusal would be a violation of contract, and then we would be back to our villages. Without bond."

The villages of Gubam were hardscrabble affairs indeed, the villagers no more than serfs, bonded to the land. Even that was still better than being unbonded, without any tie to the land. Life expectancies for the unbonded were not high.

It was Maki's turn to shudder. "All right, all right. Wulkguni have pity on us."

The oath from the agnostic Maki took Pindan by surprise. To his raised eyebrow, Maki just shrugged and shook his head.

Maki reported back a couple days later. It was clear he had spent most of that time in interface, running on "machine time", about 30:1 subjective. He looked mentally exhausted, like he had spent sleepless months working on the problem. As, in effect, he had.

"Well, the mental interface itself is no problem, of course, even for people who have never interfaced before. We just use the interface training program that we use on people when they join the civil service. And it turns out to be a lot easier to execute sentence than I thought. Too easy. It's more a case of taking protections out than of putting anything in. This memory business is proving to be the big problem."

"How so?"

"Well, what is the reliability of memories, really? What's true and what isn't? We know that people's reported memories are not very reliable in matching reality. Is that because their senses themselves are unreliable? Is it because, of all the sensory data coming into the brain every second, the individual actually only pays attention to a very small part of it? Is it stored in a faulty way, where the person's character and biases and personality filter what actually gets saved? Or do people modify the data once stored, edit their memories over time, to match their worldview?

"And that's not all. Maybe the senses and the memory themselves are completely reliable. Maybe the storage, too, is completely reliable."

"How can that be so if people's memories are not reliable?" Pindan asked.

"People's *reported* memories are not reliable. Their actual data storage could be 100% reliable, but they build in access filters over time. In that case, the errors aren't in the storage, but are introduced in the way the memories are accessed. The person doesn't want to remember what actually happened, but some other version, in which they are smarter, wiser, more moral, more compassionate, more innocent than they really were."

"I can see where that would make judgment difficult," Pindan agreed.

"Oh, but it's not just missing the guilty. What if someone's the sort who normally feels guilty about the weather. No matter what goes wrong, they caused it. They could have tried harder to prevent it, so the fact that it happened anyway is somehow their fault. Over time, they may see themselves more and more as having taken an active role in something they had nothing to do with, even opposed, just to fulfill their own innate sense of guilt. We could execute someone who had no part in the illegal settlement of Lahan just for feeling bad about what happened."

Pindan looked puzzled. "Are there really people like that?"

"Sure. What about Arnurna over in Kulan's group? She once apologized to me for one of *my* programming errors. Said she should have caught it, and so it was her fault. By now, she probably thinks *she* made the original error. Probably even remembers it happening that way. So how do we sort this all out?"

"Would it help if we had some actual memory stores to test with?"

"Well, we have to test against something. Right now, I have to tell you that we're flying blind. And if I can't sort out the memory issues, then that's it: I'm not doing it. Consequences or no consequences. If it's not possible, it's not possible."

"All right, Maki. I'll see what I can do about getting hold of some test data."

It was several days before Maki reported back in again. He was really strung out now, with the characteristic apparent lethargy of the programmer who had spent way too long interfaced to the machine. Like he was so unused to being in his own body that he had to think about it every time he wanted to move.

"Well, I think I have the memory issues sorted out. I dumped my own memories, and I went through them, comparing what I thought I remembered at the conscious level to what my actual stored memories accessible with the machine are. Then I compared those to things that are independently available -- public recordings, books, that sort of thing -- that I remembered seeing or reading. It looks like the storage, at the deepest level, is accurate: people filter their memories when they access them, then remember the output of those filters later. So on the memory issues, I think I have a handle on that.

"Now I'm researching the legal issues. What's 'guilty' mean, anyway? What's 'guilty of complicity'? Do you have any idea how fuzzy those seemingly clear-cut ideas can be in the law? I've finally begun to make sense of it, and there are a number of factors I need to take into account." He ticked them off on his fingers as he spoke.

"One, did the person know the settlement was illegal? Did they even know they were going to Lahan? Say you're some poor bastard in one of the villages -- and they're no better on Wurrpbu and Kornu than they are on Gubam, believe me; probably worse, in fact -- and someone comes up to you and offers you your own land, better climate, free seed and equipment, and no indentured serfdom? You gonna ask questions, or you gonna jump on that ship before they change their mind? Same thing with the spacers, and the merchants who provided supplies, and the soldiers who garrisoned the colony, and all the rest. Did they know what was going on? Did they know it was illegal?

"Two, did the person have any choice? Were they just ordered to do whatever, or did they choose to? I'm not sure how many of the participants were volunteers, but from what I know of the setup there it's not much different than here. 'Thank you for volunteering' is the first thing you know about it. Same thing with the military people and the commercial spacers who protected or transported the colony. How much choice did they have?"

"Not much, I guess," Pindan agreed.

"Exactly. But now there's the other side. How about someone who had no choice anyway, but he actively supported the project, came up with some additional ideas on how to make it work or whatever? So he knows it's illegal, but he doesn't have any choice in the matter, but if he did, he'd probably have supported it. And he worked harder than he needed to in order to make it successful. That's got to count against him as well.

"The other side of that coin is the guy who had no choice, but did in fact oppose the project. He maybe filed a protest to his orders as a military man, or dragged his feet on going along with the thing as much as he could without being shot or tried for treason. That's certainly got to count in his favor."

"I can see that as well," Pindan said, nodding.

"Right. So the problem is, in real cases, it's probably some combination of the four, in varying degrees. The guy who opposed it, and then got excited about seeing it work once it was underway, or the guy who didn't know what was going on, but then was enthusiastic for it once he figured it out, or the guy who just went along with orders, but then got more and more concerned and actively started working against the project, or, or, or. How do I balance all the factors for real cases?"

"I can see the problem." Pindan leaned back, recalling his orders. "The goal is not to let anyone get away who was 'complicit', so I think that means they have to have knowledge. Probably also have to have supported the project in some material way, some action they took, not just said 'Wow, that's great' and then went about their other business. The other thing that I know from our orders is that the Alliance wants to make an example, and they don't want anyone left who would make a similar decision again given the same circumstances. We came awfully close to being right back into a multi-axis space war before the Captain and a couple of the other planets forced the Alliance on everyone. I understand we were pretty close to the brink on this one."

"Understood. It's just not as easy as everyone thinks, that's all."

"Well, that's why they gave it to us."

"Yeah. Sure. I'm honored and all that. I still don't know how to balance all the factors, come up with anything approaching a true legal judgment. I still don't know this thing is really possible, and I won't until I get to cases. When are we going to have some real data?"

"Any time. I understand that some people have been judged guilty already by other means, and have lost their privacy rights. Some others waived their privacy rights so we could have the data. They must think that going through their memories will exonerate them where the externally available facts would be incriminating."

"Well, when you give me the data, can you make sure that they aren't sorted into those two groups? I want to go through them without any preconceptions. I don't want to be biased by any externals."

"I'll take care of it, Maki. And get some rest will you? It's not good to spend so much time in interface. You don't look well."

"I'll be fine, I'll be fine. But if I'm going to do this, I have to get it right."

It was over a week later when Pindan saw Maki again. He was shocked by the programmer's condition. He staggered and jerked, like a man who had forgotten how to use his body, forgotten how the controls for his own muscles worked. His speech was soft and slurred, and he spoke in choppy partial sentences separated by pauses. He'd almost forgotten how to speak.

"It's done. Ran through the test data. All two hundred cases. Verified it manually. The judgment of the algorithm. You know, against my own judgment. The things we talked about. Some borderline cases. Not as many as I thought. Most people made up their minds. One way or the other. Had either misgivings or enthusiasm. By the time it was in full swing anyway."

"So you're happy with it?"

"No. Miserable about it. Good as I can make it."

"I've looked over the judgment file you sent me, and there were some cases I was surprised about. I wasn't surprised that most of the government ministers were in the whole thing up to their necks, on both planets, but there were some innocent verdicts that were surprising. Like Fleet Commander Burnum. I thought he supported the whole project right down the line."

"Yes and no. Loyal soldier. Career man. Thought it was a mistake. Said so in private. Filed written objection. Could have been shot. Reputation saved him. Supported it in public." Maki waved his hand to one side with an effort, dismissing the guilt of the highest military commander of Wurrpbu. "Loyal soldier. That's all."

"Ah. And some of these others? The garrison commander for the Kornu colony on Lahan? Or the head of the commercial shipping monopoly on Wurrpbu? Same thing?"

"Yeah. Caught in the gears. Poor bastards."

"All right. Well, it's a tremendous job. You're to be congratulated. But right now, let's get you down to the hospital. You don't look at all well. You shouldn't have pressed so hard."

"Owed it to them. Owed it to myself. Had to be right. Had to."

Pindan took the call from the Executive Officer -- second in authority only to the Captain himself -- who acted as Gubam's minister of justice.

"I wanted to call you personally and express the Captain's Thanks for the tremendous job you did on the justice algorithm. Some of the more surprising verdicts were reviewed by our finest jurists, and they concurred with the machine's judgment in every case. A tremendous piece of both legal research and programming, and you did it fast enough for us to head off another attempt by some of the more militant Alliance members to simply kill everyone on Kornu and Wurrpbu. The Captain does not wish the blood of planets on his hands. You have saved his honor, and that of Gubam."

"Thank you, Excellency, but I did not do the programming. The entire programming task was done by Maki. All of the work is his; I can take no credit, sir."

"An honorable admission. I need to speak to Maki, then. He has the Captain's Thanks, and will be named a Hero of the Captaincy of Gubam. Please summon him to this call."

"I'm sorry, I can't do that, Excellency. In this case, the Hero of the Captaincy will have to be awarded posthumously, I'm afraid."

"*What?*"

"This job, well, it ate him up, sir. Destroyed his body. Destroyed his mind, for that matter. Destroyed him utterly.

"The only thing left intact was his honor."

Honor Restored

The beggar shuffled forward as the queue inched along. Everyone in the small town, from banker to baker to beggar, had been lined up under the watchful eyes of the Alliance ground troops. Now they awaited their trials before the judgment computer, which would determine the extent to which each held responsibility for Wurrpbu's ill-fated effort to colonize Lahan in violation of the Treaty of Ngurrun. Across all the islands of the planet Wurrpbu, the entire population was subject to the trials.

The penalty for complicity was death.

"Next!" Now at the front of the line, the beggar shuffled forward, and was escorted under guard through the gate in the fence around the square and into the town hall. He was led into a small, anonymous room and directed to sit in a chair before a desk behind which sat a clerk of the trials. The guard remained in the room, weapon at low ready, standing to the beggar's right, where the clerk would be out of his line of fire. The damage to the wall on the beggar's left, and the stains on the floor, showed that this was not an unwarranted precaution.

"Name?" the clerk asked in a bored tone.

"Wirril Jurlak," the beggar mumbled.

The clerk got an abstracted look as she consulted the records through her mental interface to the judgment computer in the sleek Alliance gunboat behind the building.

"*Wing Commander* Wirril Jurlak?" The clerk shot a glance to the guard, who stiffened and brought his weapon up to train it on the beggar.

"Yes. I was -- discharged."

"Dishonorably discharged, correct? For desertion and cowardice?"

The beggar had been hunched, looking down at his feet. Now he visibly shrank further into the chair in his shame.

"Yes."

The clerk shrugged. "Wirril Jurlak, you may enter a plea of guilty or not guilty of complicity in the illegal settlement of Lahan by Wurrpbu in violation of the Treaty of Ngurrun. If you plead not guilty, in your defense you must subject yourself to an inspection of your memories by the judgment computer. If you are found guilty by the judgment computer, the computer itself will terminate your mental processes and you will die here, now, in that chair. If you are found innocent, you will be freed and allowed to go back about your business. In either case, the computer will retain no record of your memories, and your memories will not be exposed to any other person or computer at any time. If you object to this inspection, or if you enter a plea of guilty, you will be executed for complicity immediately. Do you understand your rights?"

"Yes."

"How do you plead?"

The guard, at the ready, stiffened as the beggar straightened and looked the clerk in the eye. Some of his former status came into his voice as he answered. "Not guilty."

"Very well. Your military position will have given you experience in mental computer interfacing, so we need not instruct you in that regard. You will now subject yourself to judgment."

The beggar nodded and closed his eyes. He reached out to the judgment computer in his mind, and lowered his mental barriers to complete domination by the machine. The memories he had suppressed for so long flooded back, flashing through his mind as the judgment computer accessed the evidence.

Wing Commander Jurlak, your orders are to escort the First Settlement Convoy to Lahan.... Jurlak, following the orders of Wurrpbu Fleet Command is not optional.... Wing Commander Jurlak, you have been charged with refusing the lawful command of a superior officer. How do you plead?... Wing Commander Jurlak, you have been found guilty of desertion and cowardice.... Due to your rank and past military service, you have been spared the death penalty....

Wirril Jurlak opened his eyes with the once-familiar disorientation of emerging from the machine. His eyes came back into focus on the clerk of the trials, behind the desk in the small room in the town hall. The clerk looked surprised.

"Wirril Jurlak, you have been found innocent of complicity in the illegal settlement of Lahan by Wurrpbu in violation of the Treaty of Ngurrun. You have the right to receive a computer-readable implant documenting your innocence as you depart the building. Thank you for cooperating with the trials. You are free to go."

Wirril Jurlak, hero, traitor, convict, beggar, freed from the trials and from his shame, strode out of the door of the town hall into the red-yellow afternoon sunlight of Wurrpbu.

RICHARD F. WEYAND

www.ingramcontent.com/pod-product-compliance
Lightning Source LLC
Chambersburg PA
CBHW070552180626
46817CB00005B/1800